A New York Public Library 100 Books for Reading and Sharing selection

A Chicago Public Library Best of the Best selection

"Irresistible."
—Detroit News

★ "This second foray is even more enjoyable than the author's acclaimed debut."
—Publishers Weekly, starred review

"...book begs to be read aloud, preferably to children who delight equally in hearing about pools of vomit and blood and about triumphant heroes."
—School Library Journal,
STARRED REVIEW

"Adam Gidwitz's Grimm outlook will delight kids."
—Pittsburgh Post-Gazette

Fairy tales were, in a word, *horrible*.

Two hundred years ago, in Germany, the Brothers Grimm first wrote down that version of Cinderella in which the stepsisters slice off pieces of their feet and get their eyes pecked out. In England, a man named Joseph Jacobs collected tales like Jack the Giant Killer, which is about a boy named Jack who goes around murdering giants in the most gruesome and grotesque ways imaginable. And there was this guy called Hans Christian Andersen, who lived in Denmark and wrote fairy tales filled with sadness and humiliation and loneliness. Even Mother Goose's rhymes could get pretty dark—after all, Jack and Jill go up a hill, and then Jack falls down and **breaks his head open.**

Yes, fairy tales were horrible. In the original sense of the word.

But even these horrible fairy tales and nursery rhymes aren't **true.** They're just stories. Right?

Not exactly.

ALSO BY
Adam Gidwitz

A Tale Dark & Grimm
The Grimm Conclusion

PUFFIN BOOKS
An Imprint of Penguin Group (USA) Inc.

A COMPANION TO A TALE DARK & GRIMM

IN A GLASS GRIMMLY

ADAM GIDWITZ

PUFFIN BOOKS
An imprint of Penguin Young Readers Group
Published by the Penguin Group
Penguin Group (USA) Inc.
375 Hudson Street
New York, New York 10014, U.S.A.

USA / Canada / UK / Ireland / Australia / New Zealand / India / South Africa / China
Penguin Books Ltd, Registered Offices: 80 Strand, London WC2R 0RL, England

For more information about the Penguin Group visit www.penguin.com

First published in the United States of America by Dutton Children's Books, 2012
Published by Puffin Books, an imprint of Penguin Young Readers Group, 2013

THE LIBRARY OF CONGRESS HAS CATALOGED THE DUTTON CHILDREN'S BOOKS EDITION AS FOLLOWS:
Gidwitz, Adam.
In a glass Grimmly / Adam Gidwitz.—1st ed.
p. cm.
Summary: Companion to A tale dark & Grimm.
Summary: Frog joins cousins Jack and Jill in leaving their own stories to seek a magic mirror,
encountering such creatures as giants, mermaids, and goblins along the way. Based in part on fairy
tales from the Brothers Grimm and Hans Christian Andersen.
ISBN 978-0-525-42581-6 (hardback)
[1. Fairy tales. 2. Characters in literature—Fiction. 3. Frogs—Fiction. 4. Cousins—Fiction.
5. Adventure and adventurers—Fiction. 6. Humorous stories.] I. Grimm, Jacob, 1785–1863.
II. Grimm, Wilhelm, 1786–1859. III. Mother Goose. IV. Title.
PZ8.G36In 2012
[Fic]—dc23 2012015515

Puffin Books ISBN 978-0-14-242506-0

Creative Direction by *Deborah Kaplan*   Designed by *Irene Vandervoort*

Printed in the United States of America

3 5 7 9 10 8 6 4 2

The publisher does not have any control over and does not assume
any responsibility for author or third-party websites or their content.

To Lauren—
My inspiration,
my motivation, my home.

We see now as in a glass, grimmly.

But then we shall see face to face.

Contents

Once upon a time, fairy tales were horrible.

Not *boring* horrible. Not *so-cute-you-want-to-jump-out-the-window* horrible.

Horrible like they define it in the dictionary:

Horrible (adj.)—causing feelings of horror, dread, unbearable sadness, and nausea; also tending to produce nightmares, whimpering for one's parents, and bed-wetting.

I know, I know. You're thinking: "Fairy tales? Horrible? *Please*." I get that.

If you've been raised on the drivel that passes for fairy tales these days, you're not going to believe a word that I'm saying.

First of all, you're probably used to hearing the same boring fairy tales over and over and over again. "Today, children, we're going to read a Cinderella story from China! Today, children, we're going to read a Cinderella story from Madagascar! Today, children, we're going to read a Cinderella story from the Moon! Today, children—"

Second of all, those fairy tales that you hear over and over and over again aren't even the *real* fairy tales. Has your teacher ever said to you, "Today, children, we're going to read a Cinderella story where the stepsisters cut off their toes and their heels with a butcher's knife! And then they get their eyes pecked out by birds! Ready? Is everyone sitting crisscross-applesauce?"

No? She's never said that?

I didn't think so.

But that's what the real fairy tales are like: strange, bloody, and horrible.

Two hundred years ago, in Germany, the Brothers Grimm first wrote down that version of Cinderella in which the stepsisters slice off pieces of their feet and get their eyes pecked out. In England, a man named Joseph Jacobs collected tales like Jack the Giant Killer, which is about a boy named Jack who goes around murdering giants in the most gruesome and grotesque ways imaginable. And there was this guy called Hans Christian Andersen, who lived in Denmark and wrote fairy tales filled with sadness and humiliation and loneliness. Even Mother Goose's rhymes could get pretty dark—after all, Jack and Jill go up a hill, and then Jack falls down and *breaks his head open.*

Yes, fairy tales were horrible. In the original sense of the word.

But even these horrible fairy tales and nursery rhymes aren't *true.* They're just stories. Right?

Not exactly.

You see, buried in these rhymes and tales are true stories, of true children, who fought through the darkest times, and came out the other end—stronger, braver, and, usually, completely covered in blood.

This book is the tale of two such children: a boy named Jack, and a girl named Jill. Yes, they do fall down a hill at one point. And yes, Jack does break his head wide open.

But there is more than that. There is a beanstalk. There are giants. There might even be a mermaid or two.

Their story is terrifying. It is revolting. It is horrible.

It is the most horrible fairy tale I have ever heard.

Also, it is beautiful. Not sweet. Not cute. Beautiful—like

the gray and golden ashes in a fireplace. Or like the deep russet of a drying stain of blood.

And, best of all, it is true.

Now, let me just say that if you happen to be the kind of person who actually likes cute and sweet fairy tales, or the kind of person who thinks children should not read about decapitation and dismemberment, or, finally, if you're the kind of person who, upon hearing about two children wading through a pool of blood and vomit, runs out of the room screaming, you don't need to worry. This book is for you. There is no decapitation, dismemberment, people without clothing, or pools of blood and vomit anywhere in this book.

At least, not anywhere in the first few pages.

"Wait!" you're probably asking. "What was that about people without clothing?"

Nothing! Moving right along!

CHAPTER ONE

The
Wishing Well

O nce upon a time, there was a kingdom called Märchen, which sat just next to the modern countries of England, Denmark, and Germany.

I need to interrupt. Already. I apologize. No one in the history of the world has ever pronounced the word "Märchen" correctly. Some people say *Marchin'*, like what the ants go doing if you're from Texas.

That's not right.

Some people say *MARE-chen*. That's closer, but still wrong.

Others say **MARE-shen**. That's about as close as I've ever gotten to pronouncing it right, so it's probably good enough for you, too.

But if you really want to say the name of the kingdom that this story takes place in correctly (and I don't know why you would, I'm just offering, because I'm nice like that), you've got to say MARE, then you've got to make a sound in your throat like you're hocking a loogie, and then you have to say *shen*. Like this: **MARE-cccch-shen**.

You know what? You might just want to say *Marchin'*.

At the center of the kingdom Märchen was a castle. Behind this castle was a hidden grove. In the grove was a well. And at the bottom of the well there lived a frog.

He was a sad frog. He did not like his well. It was wet and mossy and dirty, and very very very very very very very smelly.

All day long the frog sat at the bottom of his well as salamanders splashed around him. Now, maybe you know it, and maybe you don't, but salamanders are not the most *popular* creatures in the animal kingdom.

But why? Salamanders seem all right to you. They're lots of pretty colors, like shimmery purple and glowy red. They have tiny black eyes that stare at you oh-so-very-cutely. And they have these little mouths that are permanently curled into tiny, maybe-smiles.

All of this is true. But, in addition to the pretty colors and the tiny eyes and the maybe-smiles, they have these shrill little voices which they use to ask the most idiotic, mind-numbing questions that you have ever heard.

For example:

"Why is blue?"

Or, "Who is a stone?"

Or, "What tastes better, a fly or a fly?"

Or, "Who is uglier, me or Fred? Is it me? It's me, right? Me? Is it me?"

The sad frog's only solace, amid the damp, and the filth, and the smell, and the salamanders, was the sky. All day and all night, the frog stared up at a little patch of sky that peered down into his clearing. Sometimes it was gray like slate, other times it was inky black, other times it was washed with a burning red. But most of the time the sky above his well was a clear, deep blue, with white shapes like fluffy rocks that floated across its face. All day and all night he stared up, unblinking, at that sky.

And then, one day, while the frog was staring up at his sky, he heard a peculiar *stomp-stomp-stomping* on the forest floor. It was followed by a sudden *whoomp*, and then a cry. Curious, he climbed the slippery stone wall to the top of his well and peered out.

Sitting on the forest floor, with matted hair and muddied clothes, was a little girl. Her face was red with anger and exertion. Her lips were all scrunched up and furious. But her eyes . . . The frog studied them. Her eyes . . . Well, her eyes looked just like the patch of sky above his well when it was its clearest, deepest blue.

"They *can't* play with my ball!" the little girl bellowed at no one in particular. "They *can't*. It's *mine!*" She began to throw the ball up and down, glancing over her shoulder from time to time to see if she had been followed into the wood, and returning, disappointed, to her ball each time she discovered she had not been.

The frog watched, mesmerized. And where you or I might have begun to suspect this little girl of being a selfish brat, the frog, not knowing many (any) humans, saw only a maiden who had somehow captured the sky and kept it jailed behind her eyelids. And he suddenly felt that if only he could spend the rest of his days in the presence of this beautiful creature he would be perfectly and totally happy.

So the frog began to croak at the top of his lungs. *Maybe she'll notice me!* he thought. And then he thought, *Maybe she'll take me home with her!* And then he thought, *Wait, she doesn't live with salamanders!* And so he put every ounce of hope that flowed through his froggy little veins into each expert amphibian warble.

ADAM GIDWITZ

But, of course, the girl did not notice him. She only threw her ball up and down, up and down. The frog sat there croaking for a full hour, but never once did she look at him. Finally, she stood up and took her ball out of the wood. The frog, in despair, threw himself from the edge of his well, down to the depths, hoping that the long fall would kill him. It didn't. Instead, the salamanders began to nudge him with their blunt noses.

"Hey! Hey! Hey!"

"Are you dead?"

"Are you? Frog? Frog?"

"What is it like to be dead?"

"Am I dead?"

"Am I smelly?"

"Who's smellier, me or Fred? Me? It's me, right?"

The frog shoved moss into his ear holes.

But, to the frog's great joy, the girl returned to the wood to play with her ball the next day, and the day after, and the day after that. And every day, the frog wooed her with the most magnificent croaks he could muster. But she never noticed him. Still, he took pleasure in watching her, examining her utterly perfect beauty, and imagining all the happy times they might one day spend together.

———

Alas, dear reader, you know as well as I do the mistake that our poor friend, the frog, is making. We all know that beauty is well and fine, but that it is unimportant when compared to questions of goodness, kindness, intelligence, and honesty. And, watching the girl throwing her ball in the air, the frog could determine nothing of these things. In fact, he knew next to nothing about her.

He did not know that this wasn't just any little girl he had fallen in love with. She was the princess, the king's only daughter. He also did not know that, as pretty as she was, she was a horror. Sweet and pretty on the outside, cruel and selfish on the inside.

If you know anything about children, dear reader, perhaps this will not surprise you. Perhaps you know that one of the greatest dangers in life is growing up very pretty.

You see, when you are very pretty, people tend to remark on your looks. They smile at you more easily. They are more permissive of your faults. Soon, you come to believe that your prettiness matters, and that you are better because you are pretty, and that all it takes to get through life is a batting of your eyelashes and a twisting of your hair around your little finger, and that you can scream and pout and shout and tease because everyone will still like you anyway because you are so unbelievably pretty. This is what many very pretty people think.

Beware, then, for this is how monsters are made.

And I fear that our poor frog has fallen in love with a pretty little monster.

One day, the girl came to the well rather later than usual. As she played with her ball in the small clearing, the sun began to set, and the edges of twilight rose like a black mist in the east. The darkness made it harder to see the ball, and so, on one particular toss, the princess missed it, and it bounced directly into the well.

The girl yelped and ran to the well's edge. She peered down into the dark. The frog, who had never been so close to the girl, stared at her and tried not to hyperventilate.

Suddenly, the girl began to wail like a foghorn. She wailed and wailed and wept and wailed some more. Well, it pained the frog to see her like that. He croaked at her, trying to comfort her, but she paid no attention to him.

Oh, if only she could hear me! he thought. *If only she knew I was trying to help her!*

As the girl wept into the darkness of the well, tears ran down her face, dropped from her dimpled chin, and splashed into the black water below.

Far up above, the first few stars had just begun to appear in the sky. The tears that fell into the well shook the surface of the water, and with it, the stars' reflection. Now maybe you know it, and maybe you don't, but this is the only way to wake the stars. And awake they did.

Meanwhile, the frog was trying with all his might to croak something that the girl might understand. "I can get your ball!" he tried to tell her. "I can help you, beautiful, radiant, perfectly nonamphibious creature!" And as he stared into her cerulean eyes, now fading to gray in the dying light, he went beyond wanting to help her, and even beyond longing to help her. He wished for it, in loud, croaking, frog-wishing sounds.

Well, the stars heard his wish, and they granted it.

What? The stars *heard* the frog?

 And they grant wishes?

 Yes, they did.

 And yes, they do.

———

       ADAM GIDWITZ

Without any warning, his croaks became perfectly comprehensible to the girl, and what had before been, *"Ribbit . . . ribbit . . . ribbit . . . "* became, "Please, beautiful girl, let me help you!"

The girl stood up like a bolt. "Who said that?" she asked.

"I think I did," said the frog, as surprised as she was.

"You can talk?" she asked.

"Apparently," he replied, bemused. "I . . . I was offering to help you."

"Oh, *would* you?!" she cried, and the frog nearly fell to pieces. "Oh, I would do *anything*! Really I would! Just get my ball and I'll give you *anything*! You can have my jewels, or my fanciest clothes, or my crown . . ."

Your crown? the frog thought, but he didn't say it. He hadn't known that she was a princess. But of course, upon examining her again, what else could she have been?

With all the gallantry he could muster, the frog replied, "Of course I'll get it! You don't have to give me anything . . ." He stopped. Her mouth—looking like an unbloomed rose—had moved just slightly as he spoke, and his emotions began to betray him. He stammered, and turned a brighter shade of green. "Umm . . ." he muttered. "Unless . . ." he stammered. "You could always . . ." he stuttered.

"Anything!" the princess said. "I'll give you anything!"

"I was just thinking . . . that we might be friends . . ."

"Oh, of *course* we'll be friends!" the princess said. "I think we'll be *ever* so close, if you would just fetch my ball!"

Well, the princess didn't mean it, of course. It was just something nice you were supposed to say to lowly people (and, apparently, to frogs) so as not to hurt their feelings. She had learned all about not hurting people's feelings *ages* ago.

But the frog, not having met many (any) humans, didn't understand that. And he, poor frog, believed her. So, with a brimming heart, he dove into the depths of the well and brought up the princess's ball. She instantly grabbed it, shouted with joy, said, "Oh *thank* you, frog!" and immediately ran toward the castle. The frog, who had expected to spend a bit more time with her, now that they were *ever* so close, hopped down from the well and tried to follow her.

"Wait!" he shouted, "wait for me! I can't keep up!" But of course, the princess did not wait for him. She pretended she could not hear him.

Later that night, the king sat at dinner with his daughter. As they ate their salad course, the quiet was broken by a faint *splish-splash splish-splash*, coming from just under the windows. Then it seemed to start up the stairs. The princess went deathly white.

There was a pause, and then there came a knocking on the door.

"What's that?" the king asked.

"What? I don't hear anything," said the princess.

The knocking continued.

"That!" said the king.

But the princess had already leaped from her chair and rushed to the front door.

She opened it a crack. There, waiting wet and expectant on the doorstep, was the frog. She slammed the door and returned to the dinner table.

The king examined her pale features. "Who was it, my dear?" he asked.

"Oh, nobody," she said, and shoveled far too much salad into her mouth so as not to be able to say any more. The knocking came again.

"It *is* someone," the king insisted. "Who is it?"

The princess burst into tears. "He's an awful, ugly old frog!" she cried. "He fetched my ball for me when it was lost in the well, and I told him he could be my friend! Oh, it's terrible!" The princess's wails echoed off the ceiling. "*Waaaaaaaaaaaoooooooooooooooh!*"

The king, who had learned long ago that the princess could

turn her tears on and off whenever she wanted to, insisted that she open the door and bring the creature in.

Meanwhile, the frog nervously knocked at the door again. Perhaps, he thought, the princess hadn't seen him when she opened the door. He was rather small, of course. Easy to overlook. He repeated this to himself, attempting to cover up a deeper fear that she had, in fact, seen him, and slammed the door because of it.

But his fears were allayed when the door opened again and the princess appeared. He broke into his broadest frog-grin and said, "Good evening, Princess. I was just passing by, and I thought I might stop in to call upon you. Is this a convenient time?" He had rehearsed this speech during the three hours it took him to hop from his well to the castle's door.

"Well, it isn't really . . ." said the princess, and she began to close the door again, when, from the dining room, the king bellowed, "Invite him to dinner!"

The princess scowled.

The frog's heart swelled as he saw the stunning hall, the servants lined up against the walls, the glorious dining table, and the king—the king!—seated at its head. The king was very polite to him and offered him a chair. But the frog was too short to get up into it. "Pick him up," the king commanded his daughter.

The frog's heart began to flutter. She was going to touch him! He pictured her delicate fingers, lifting him into the air. He sighed in anticipation.

Abruptly, he was dangling from one foot, and, just as abruptly, dropped onto the hard wood of a chair. He looked up. The princess was grimacing. "I need to wash my hands now, Daddy," she said.

Humiliation swept over the frog.

"Really," said the frog, "I am quite clean. It's those dreadful salamanders who give us well-dwellers a bad name."

But the princess was already washing her hands in a bowl brought over by a servant. The frog sat awkwardly on his chair for a while. He certainly couldn't reach the table—he couldn't even see if there was food on it to eat. Presently, the king noticed this. "Honey, lift your friend up onto the table so he can have his soup." (The salad course had been finished, you see, and the soup had been brought out.)

The frog found himself suddenly lifted and plopped down on the table, and he flushed to see the princess anxiously calling for the washing bowl again. He brought his face over the steaming saucer of soup and smelled it. "Luxuriant," he said to the king. "What is it?"

The princess let out a guffaw. The king began to turn red.

Terror took hold of the frog. What had he said? The princess was laughing loudly and cruelly now. He couldn't think of *what* he had done wrong. He looked imploringly at the beautiful girl.

"It's frog's leg soup!" she cried, laughing and pointing. Servants stifled their laughter behind their hands. The king, though, was deeply embarrassed.

"Take this away!" he cried. Presently, other food was brought, though the frog had entirely lost his appetite. A few times he tried to engage the table in conversation, but each time the princess snickered or insulted him. By the end of dinner, he was on the verge of tears. His dreams of a new life with the sky-eyed princess were dead.

"I am tired," he said. "Perhaps I should go."

"Perhaps you should," the princess agreed.

But the king said, "Take him with you upstairs. He can sleep on a pillow in your room; certainly you won't make him walk—hop—all the way home in the dark. A weasel might get him."

"I wouldn't care!" the princess announced. "And I'm not touching him again!" A few of the servants chortled, and the frog wished that he had never made his stupid wish. But wishes cannot be unwished, no matter how one wishes it. A wish is a powerful thing. It had the frog in its grip. And it was not about to let him go.

ADAM GIDWITZ

Finally, the king convinced his daughter (through threats and imprecations) to take the poor frog upstairs. She did this as quickly as she could, holding him by a single leg and bouncing him as she climbed the long, winding staircases. He was afraid he might come to pieces. (*Though then they could use me in the soup*, he thought bitterly.) As he watched the little girl, he marveled at her lack of feeling, and also at her beautiful, deep blue eyes. *If only she would like me*, he thought. *If only . . .*

They reached her room, and she dropped him to the floor and went into her washroom to prepare for bed. When she emerged, she found him huddled in a damp corner, trying in vain to pretend he was at home, at the bottom of his loathed well. *At least it was better than this*, he thought.

She approached him, and he shivered with fear. But her face had changed. It was softer. Maybe even sympathetic. Hope blossomed in his little chest.

Gently, she reached down and took him under his belly. He shivered.

She lifted him up, so he was near her face. He stared at her rose-lips, and into her cerulean eyes.

And she kissed him.

———

Right?

That's what happens now, doesn't it?

Of course not. What sense would that make?

As anyone who's read the Brothers Grimm would know, this is actually when she throws him against a wall with all of her might in an attempt to kill him.

And only *then*, after the attempted *murder*, does he reveal himself as an enchanted prince. And then they get married. And live happily ever after.

Which is clearly idiotic. Why would they live happily ever after if she's just tried to kill him?

And why would being smashed against a wall turn him back into a prince?

And who said he was a prince in the first place?

At this point, I ought to make something clear. There are three versions of this story:

There is the kiddie version, where they kiss. Obviously false.

There is the Grimm version, where she throws him against the wall, and then they get married. Which is, if you ask me, even more ridiculous than the kiddie version.

And then there is the true version. What actually happened. Which is this:

The princess took the frog by one leg, swung him around her head, and hurled him as hard as she could at the wall of her room. But as she swung him, she held on too tight, and his little leg came off.

So the frog flew across the room and slammed into the wall. The princess found herself holding a single frog leg in her hand, screamed, and threw it out the window. Where it was eaten by a weasel.

As you might have suspected, our poor frog did not regain the form of a prince, because he had never been a prince. He was a frog. A frog in love with a beautiful, cruel princess.

Which means that being thrown against a wall hurts. In all sorts of ways.

The frog lay crumpled in a heap at the base of the wall. He was bleeding from the place where his leg had been (for when you prick frogs, they do indeed bleed), while the princess stared at him with a disgusting air of satisfaction.

With all the dignity he had left to him, the little frog hobbled out of her room, down the great stairs, and out into the night, trailing froggy blood after him as he went.

The End

My guess is that everyone's a little upset right now.

Some of you are upset because of all the horrible things that just happened to that poor frog. You like the frog. He's kind and honest and his emotions are deep and pure. And you don't like seeing him hurt. Right?

Others of you might be upset because the frog's story wasn't horrible enough. Yes, he had his heart broken, his leg torn off (and eaten by a weasel), and was hurled against a stone wall. But no one died. There were no pools of blood and vomit. Everyone had all of their clothing on.

Well, nobody should be worried.

The frog will be fine. He will be more than fine. He will be great. He will be awesome. He will be heroic.

Remember that. Repeat it and hold it close to your heart. You'll need to.

Because before that happens, this story will get more horrible. Like, way, *way* more horrible. Like, blood and vomit and no-clothing horrible.

But, through it all, the frog will be okay. That's a promise.

And Jack and Jill? Will they be okay, too?

Sure!

Sort of!

CHAPTER TWO

The Wonderful Mother

Once upon a time there was a little girl who had the most wonderful mother you could possibly imagine.

Go ahead. Try to imagine the most wonderful mother you can.

Have you?

All right. Not good enough. Not even close.

First of all, this little girl's mother was a queen. Was the mother you were thinking of a queen? If not, she's already not good enough. And we've barely begun.

Second of all, the little girl's mother was beautiful. I mean, really beautiful. Stunningly gorgeous. Her golden hair was as long and thick as you please, and hung all the way down to the curve of her back. She was tall, like a statue. And slender, like a willow wand. Her lips were rich and red like an unbloomed rose. And her eyes—well, her eyes—her eyes were a cerulean blue so clear and shining that you could stare into them for hours and never think to blink.

Of course, this mother was also wonderful in a number of other ways.

Her clothes, for example, were the absolute pinnacle of style. And her hair was just perfect—oh, wait, did I already mention her hair? Anyway, it's worth mentioning twice.

As you can see, she really was the most wonderful mother imaginable.

And her daughter knew it. How could she not?

One cold winter day, this wonderful mother sat before the looking glass in her room, and her little girl, whose name was Jill, sat beside her and watched her mother's expert hands apply red to her fine lips and pale cheeks. Jill's feet were soaking in a tub of ice water. "Beautiful women have the softest feet," her mother told her. Jill nodded fiercely and tried not to shiver so loudly that her mother could hear.

Suddenly, from the street below, they heard the cry of a poor beggar, braving the cold in search of food. "Bread!" he cried.

"Bread for a freezing old man!" The queen rolled her eyes at Jill. Little Jill smiled at her mother and, once the queen had gone back to her makeup, practiced rolling her eyes as well.

But the beggar cried out again, "Bread! Please! Can anyone spare some bread?" He must have been right below their window, for his voice bounced around the snowy eaves, through the open window, and directly into the room. Jill's mother raised her eyebrows at Jill, and then dipped her finger in a pot of rouge. The little girl practiced raising her eyebrows.

"Bread! Bread for a freezing, starving man!" the beggar cried.

"Putrid, too," the queen said. "I can practically smell him from here." Jill giggled. Her mother added, "Don't make me smile, child. I'll ruin the rouge."

"BREAD!" the beggar screamed.

"Heavens!" The queen looked at Jill in the mirror. Her eyes traveled down to the tub of ice water. Suddenly, the queen spun around, yanked the tub out from under Jill's feet, and went to the window. She stole a mischievous look over her shoulder at Jill. Jill stared, uncomprehending. Then her mother dumped the entire tub of water out of the window.

"Oh Lord!" the beggar cried. "Who did that? Oh, it's cold! It's cold!"

Jill's mother fell back into the room. Her face was contorted with hysterical, silent laughter. She looked at Jill through heaving laughs, her eyes wide, her eyebrows raised. Jill stared at her. She thought she ought to laugh, too. So she tried. Her mother began laughing harder now, the makeup on her face cracking into little caverns, her eyes wide as moons, staring at her little girl. Jill watched her mother laugh and laugh and laugh, as the beggar cried for a warm blanket in the street below.

Finally, after her fit of laughter had subsided, the queen went into her wardrobe. Jill walked over to the window. The beggar was still crying for a warm blanket. The little girl stuck her head over the sill and gazed downward. A bent, bearded man rubbed his arms up and down and begged, begged for someone to help him. Jill wondered if she could give him her shawl, or if her mother would disapprove. Probably she would disapprove.

Suddenly, the wind banged the window frames against the castle walls, rattling the glass.

The queen, from the depths of the wardrobe, cried out, "What did you break now?" Even though Jill had never broken anything of her mother's in her life.

"Nothing, Mommy!" Jill called back.

"If it's my looking glass," her mother cried, "I will never forgive you!"

Jill reached out to draw the windows closed. She looked down one last time at the beggar. Then, as she was pulling the windows in, her gaze happened to travel across the wintry square. At the opposite side, standing in the shadow of the church, were three huddled figures. They were watching Jill. Watching her with eyes that were so pale they seemed to have no color at all. Jill shivered and withdrew into the room.

Her mother was standing there, staring at her, dresses draped over her shoulders and arms and around her neck. "What's broken?" the queen snapped. "What's broken? Don't lie to me! Is it my looking glass? I must know!"

"Nothing! Nothing, Mommy, I promise!" And Jill ran to her wonderful mother and threw her arms around her and held her tightly.

What's that? You don't think she's so wonderful?

I don't know what you're talking about.

"Announcing the entrance of the world-famous Holbein Cornelius Anderson! Merchant-Adventurer and Clothier to Kings!" So read the guard. Then he stood aside, and a man, dressed in the brightest fabrics Jill had ever seen, made his way to the center of the room. He smiled from a smooth baby face, and his eyes were a blue so pale they were almost white.

It was the queen's half birthday, a holiday that the kingdom celebrated with more fervor than any other excepting the queen's actual birthday, which was a holiday so holy that even the churches were shut. "Your Majesty," the brightly clad man said with a low bow, "I am Holbein Cornelius Anderson, Merchant-Adventurer and Clothier to Kings! I have just returned from a smashingly successful trip to the East, where I made kimonos for sultans and turbans for empresses!"

The queen didn't know what a sultan or a kimono was. Her eyes narrowed. She didn't like it when people used words she didn't understand.

"But now I have returned!" Anderson went on, "And I bring with me the greatest treasure I have ever seen! And I find, lo and behold, that I return just in time for the queen's half birthday! Fate has led me to your feet, with this treasure of treasures!"

There was a pause. The king and the queen and Jill and all the courtiers in the room were silent. So was Holbein Cornelius Anderson. He looked up, right into the queen's cerulean eyes.

"Your Majesty," he said, "I bring you the finest silk, for the finest gown, in the whole entire world."

ADAM GIDWITZ

Silence again. He smiled. The queen raised an eyebrow.

"Well," she demanded impatiently, "where is it?"

"I can't show it to you here!" Anderson cried, surprised. "Your Majesty, this is the finest silk in all the world! The emperor of Japan offered me a thousand camels for it! The sultan of Arabia offered me every single buffalo he owned! The great khan, in China, offered not to cut off my head if I gave it to him! I refused them all! I wanted to save it for you, Your Majesty! Now, having traveled all these millions of miles home, I will show it to no one but you!"

"Very well," the queen announced. "Everyone leave at once! I will examine this silk alone!"

Her husband, the king, gave her a plaintive look, but she just raised an icy eyebrow at him. He, the courtiers, the guards, and the servants, all left the room. Jill was last to leave. As she was about to close the door behind her, the old merchant said, "Wait."

Jill paused and looked back.

"Princess, would you mind staying a moment?" the merchant asked. The queen raised her eyebrows at him. He ignored her. "Come in, come in, and close the door behind you," he said with a smile. Then, turning to the queen, he said, "I am sorry, Your Majesty. But you are far taller than I remembered. You see, the great queens and empresses of the East are all very small—some no taller than my knee! I knew you were taller than that, but I thought you were, perhaps, the size of the beautiful princess here. I am afraid I haven't enough silk for a dress that will fit your statuesque majesty." He looked down at the floor as if he were ashamed.

"You're going to make a dress for my *daughter*?" the queen exclaimed. "On *my* half birthday?"

"When is the princess's half birthday?" the merchant asked innocently. "Or her real birthday, for that matter? I could return then."

I have a birthday? Little Jill wondered. She thought only the queen had a birthday. She knew that she hadn't always been alive, of course, but it had never occurred to her that she—or anyone besides her mother, in fact—had been born on one specific day. It was almost a silly idea, people besides her mother having a birthday.

The queen's lovely complexion reddened, until Jill thought she might be having a heart attack like that fat lord did two Christmases ago. But her mother merely said, in a tight, clipped voice, "Let me see the silk."

The merchant nodded affably and placed his broad fabric bag before him. He opened it. He put both hands inside, moved to unfold something, and then, very slowly, drew his hands out of the bag again. He was quite the showman.

His hands were a yard apart. His fingers were pressed tightly together. His eyes ran back and forth over the distance between them. Over nothing.

"Magnificent, isn't it?" he sighed. "The most exquisite silk I have ever seen."

Jill stole a glance at her mother. The queen was staring, wide-eyed, at the empty space between his hands. Jill turned back to the merchant and mimicked her mother's facial expression exactly.

"You see it, don't you?" the merchant went on. "Only the finest eye can see silk this majestic, this perfect. I was nearly stoned to death in the kingdom of the Tartars because the king claimed that I had no silk at all. But then his wife came in and laughed in his face. You see it don't you? You see the most exquisite piece of silk that has ever been?"

"Oh, yes!" the queen said, and suddenly her voice took on a dreamy languor. "It's . . . it's wonderful. Just perfect. I didn't think there could be a silk so fine." She glanced at Jill. "Do you see it, child?"

"Oh, yes!" Jill said, echoing her mother's dreamy tone. "It's wonderful. It . . . it's wonderful." Seeing nothing, she dared say nothing more.

"The colors radiate and shine up and down the thread, do

they not?" the merchant asked. "As if a rainbow were running to keep up with the sun."

"Yes, that's just how I would describe it!" the queen exclaimed. "Like a rainbow! Or . . . or like autumn leaves, when the colors are changing!" She glanced up at the merchant hesitantly.

"Oh, Your Majesty, you are a poet! Yes, I couldn't have said it better myself!"

Jill stammered. "It's like . . . like gold pieces, kissed with the colors of sunset," she tried.

"Yes! Yes, it is!" the merchant cried, and his smile stretched across his smooth face.

"It is more like autumn leaves, Jill," said her mother coldly. "Wouldn't you say, Anderson?"

"Of course, Your Majesty," he said, folding his smile away like an apparition of silk. "But the princess has learned good taste from her mother."

"Lord knows I try," the queen sighed. Then she said, "There is not enough silk to make a gown for me?"

"Alas, Your Majesty—" the merchant replied. Jill thought she saw his pale eyes flit to hers for a moment, and in that moment there was heat, danger. But then it was gone. "Alas, no. I have just enough thread, I think, to weave a dress for the princess."

The queen, having seen the silk, did not seem so angry as she had before about not receiving the gift herself. "How long will it take?" she asked.

"If you were to give me use of a loom in the castle, and all the thread I needed, and food and drink and money for expenses, I think I could have the dress done in a month."

"A month?" the queen exclaimed. She eyed the merchant skeptically. "Make it three weeks."

"Fine," the merchant said. "But I'll have to be up all night, every night."

"Three weeks it is, then," the queen announced. "My little girl will wear the dress in the Royal Procession three weeks from today!"

Now, at this point, perhaps you think you know this story. And I'm sure you've heard some version of it, mangled and strangled and made almost sweet by years and years of telling it to little children.

But the way you know it is not the way it happened.

The real way is . . . different.

———

The very next morning, Jill climbed to the castle's highest turret. There, she found the old merchant already at work. He pumped the loom pedal with his feet as he wove the shuttle up and down, up and down. Jill stared at his hands picking nimbly at the space where the shuttle wove. There was nothing there. Nothing at all on the loom. She was sure of it.

Just then, the merchant looked up. Their eyes met. Again, she felt that heat, that danger. But just for an instant. It passed, and the merchant said, "What do you think of my work, Princess?"

She walked slowly over to the loom. His feet stopped pumping. The shuttle hovered in the air above where the material should have been. She surveyed the nothing.

Do you see it, child? the queen had asked.

Jill looked up at the merchant. "My mother was right," she said. "It is more like autumn leaves."

The merchant smiled. "Yes, my dear. Well, you can always hope to be as wise and beautiful as your mother one day. It's a worthy goal for any daughter."

Jill looked at the floor, curtsied, and turned to leave. But she ran directly into the king, who was coming to inspect the merchant's gift. He was followed by his friend and confidant, Lord Boorly.

"And where is this wonderful silk?" Lord Boorly demanded as he crossed the threshold, his monocle fixed firmly between his left eyebrow and the top of his fleshy cheek.

Then his eyes fell on the loom. His eyebrows shot up his forehead. His monocle fell to the floor and shattered. At his side, the king stared wordlessly.

"Stunning, isn't it, Your Majesty?" the merchant said.

"Uh . . ." the king began.

"The princess was just telling me that she has come to the opinion that your wife was most apt in describing this silk as like autumn leaves. Weren't you, Princess?" And he smiled at her.

"Yes," she said, studying the faces of Lord Boorly and the king curiously. "I was."

"Ah!" said Lord Boorly. "Yes! I see it now! It's hard to catch at first! So subtle! So fine! But yes! It's magnificent!" He walked up to the loom to inspect more closely. "Yes, autumn leaves—I see that. But what about peacock feathers, eh? Wouldn't you say that hits a little closer to home, Anderson?"

The merchant considered this. "It may . . ." he said at length. "It just may . . ."

The king had, by this point, come up closer to the loom. He was still inspecting it when the merchant asked him, "And you, Your Highness, what would you say it looked most like?

Lord Boorly's peacock feathers? Or your wife's leaves? Or," he added, "gold pieces kissed by the colors of sunset? That was the princess's description."

"It was, was it?" The king squinted at her, and then turned back to the loom. After a moment, he straightened up. "Well, I agree with my daughter! Gold pieces, absolutely!"

Lord Boorly looked crestfallen. "You wouldn't say peacock feathers, Your Highness?"

The king looked at Jill. She shrugged her small shoulders. He looked back at Boorly. "I most certainly would not!" he said. "Gold pieces at sunset, if anything. Leaves, maybe. But really, gold at sunset. In fact," he said, raising his voice and pointing one finger at the ceiling, "I don't think I've ever seen a color so like gold at sunset as this!" He reached out and shook the merchant's hand. "My good sir, thank you for bringing us this magnificent specimen. I cannot wait to see my daughter arrayed in such a stunning gown!" He smiled at Jill and then turned and led Lord Boorly from the room.

Jill looked at the merchant. He was staring after the two men, wonderingly, smiling. She watched him for a moment and then slipped out the door.

Jill sat in her mother's room, watching the queen sample different shades of eye shadow that had been given to her for her half birthday. After a while, she said, "Mother, can I tell you something?"

"Hmm?" replied her mother absently.

Jill studied the queen's beautiful features. "Mother, sometimes I can't see the silk."

The queen stopped dabbing at her makeup, and their eyes connected in the looking glass. Slowly, her mother said, "Sometimes?"

Jill sucked in her breath. Her mother knew. She knew Jill couldn't see it. She would be so disappointed. "Yes," Jill said hurriedly. "Sometimes I see it as if it were the brightest, most beautiful thing in the world." And then, she added quietly, "Except you."

Her mother's eyes slid back to the mirror. She *did* look disappointed. Her voice was flat when she said, "Well, perhaps one day you'll learn to see it all the time. It takes a truly refined eye."

The next day, Jill returned to the turret room. The merchant was still working away at the invisible silk, pumping and picking and weaving. Jill watched him from the doorway. After a while, he looked up.

"Ah, Princess! A pleasure to see you!" he said. "Come, come, look what I'm working on now!" Jill approached. "It's the hem!" he said. "Can't you see it? Along the edge, I'm running a slightly different color—something like the red mud at the banks of a yellow river. Do you see?"

Jill stared. She saw nothing. She hesitated.

At last, she said, "Yes."

The merchant looked up from the loom. His eyes were so pale. "Do you see it, Jill?"

Jill shivered. Then she heard her mother say, *Perhaps one day you'll learn to see it all the time.*

"Of course I can," she told the merchant. Then she left.

At last, the day came. Jill was woken very, very early in the morning to help her mother bathe. As she rubbed the bath oils and soap into her mother's smooth skin, she said, "Mother, do you think I will look beautiful today?"

The soapy water, lapping gently against the edge of the tub, was the only sound in the room. Then, slowly, the queen turned to her daughter. Jill could see her mother's eyes working up and down her face. At last, the queen said, "Perhaps you will." And she smiled.

Jill's heart sang.

———

ADAM GIDWITZ

After Jill had bathed herself, the merchant came into her dressing room. He held his hands out wide before him. He beamed. He looked at the space between his hands, and then back at Jill.

"Well?" he said, "what do you think?"

Jill stared. She saw nothing.

"I . . ." she began. Then she stopped.

"Yes?" the merchant said, frowning.

"I don't . . ." she said again.

His frown deepened. "Go on . . ."

She opened her mouth to speak. And then, in her mind, she heard the words, *Perhaps you will.*

And she said, "Will you help me put it on?"

The merchant smiled. "Of course, Your Highness."

He did not look at her when she dropped her towel. His voice was as tight as his eyelids when he said, "No underclothes, Your Highness. The silk will bunch up around it."

Slowly, with eyes closed, the merchant lowered the dress over Jill's head. "Light as air, isn't it?" he asked wistfully. She nodded and swallowed. Her eyes, too, were closed, and she concentrated on how beautiful her mother always looked, how graceful and lovely she was.

And then Jill opened her eyes and looked at herself in the mirror.

She caught her breath. A silken gown, as fine and shimmering as any that has ever been, hung weightless over her slender little shoulders. It was red and orange and blue and yellow, just exactly like a glittering, sun-dappled pile of coins as the sky is fading from pink to black. Just so did the colors of the dress blend in and out, yellow fading to orange fading to red and back again as the dress shifted over Jill's little body.

Jill clutched her hands to her chest. She had been right. Somehow, she had known just what it looked like. And her mother had been right. She did look beautiful. She knew she did.

She smiled at Holbein Cornelius Anderson in the mirror. "It's very beautiful," she said, beaming. "Thank you."

The silk merchant suddenly looked confused.

The Royal Procession started at the gate of the castle. At its head were the trumpeters, blowing the fanfare to announce the royal party. Behind them, Lord Boorly led the group of the king's and queen's most favored courtiers, arrayed in their finest clothes. Behind them walked the soldiers in their silver armor, *clomp clomp clomp*. Then came the king and the queen, arm in arm. The king wore his purple ermine. But, of course, no one noticed him. For the queen walked beside him, wearing a stunning gown of aubergine and white lace. Garnets hung around her neck and rubies from her soft earlobes. Her pale skin shined, and her blue eyes echoed the immensity of the sky.

And then, behind them, came Jill. Little Jill. Her hair had been coiffed. Her nails had been painted. She wore clay-red shoes and red ribbons in her hair. Her silk dress—so light, so smooth, so shining—swished against her legs. She felt like she was wearing one of those mirages that appear on the road on a hot day—the dress was that light, that shimmering.

The royal party entered the roaring, adoring throng that lined the streets outside the castle. The trumpets blared and the people cheered. Lord Boorly and the other courtiers waved, and the crowd whistled and waved back. The king and queen smiled serenely at their subjects, and the people of the kingdom cheered like mad.

And then they saw the princess.

A hush fell over the crowd. It ran down the street like a shiver. No one spoke. They watched the princess walking, head held high, brows arched just as the queen's always were, smiling and looking not quite at the crowd, but just above their heads.

Suddenly, a whisper shook the stillness. *"The princess's new dress! The princess's new dress!"* Jill heard it. Her smile grew a little wider. A little more confident. The whispers grew. *"The princess's new dress! Beautiful! Beautiful!"* Princess Jill allowed her head to float just a little higher. Her bearing became more natural, more regal. She stopped looking above her subjects' heads and started looking into their wondering faces. She smiled more broadly.

The whisper become a wave—"The dress is beautiful! *She* is beautiful!"—undulating through the admiring crowd. She was certain her mother could hear it, too. Jill's chest swelled near to bursting.

And then Jill noticed a little child, sitting atop her father's shoulders. The child was just a year or two younger than Jill. She even looked like Jill, a little. Similar hair. Something in the eyes, perhaps. And then Jill noticed that the little girl was staring at her strangely. Her little mouth was hanging open. Her eyebrows were crawling up her tender, rounded forehead. She raised a little finger and pointed at Jill. The smile left Jill's face.

"Why is the princess naked, Daddy?"

Jill stopped walking.

The wave of whispers faltered, then died.

"She's naked, Daddy! Why?" the child said.

The blood rushed to Jill's cheeks. She dimly perceived that, ahead of her, the procession had stopped. Her parents had turned to look at her.

"The princess is naked!" someone in the crowd cried. "The princess is naked!"

Jill looked down at herself. The reds, the yellows, the blues—were gone. There was nothing. She was, indeed, completely naked.

Jill looked up. Her mother was there. The queen's eyes were furiously wide, her nostrils flared like a bull's. Her lips were moving, but it was as if Jill had gone deaf. The world was suddenly silent, dream-like. She tried to make out what her mother was saying. Then, suddenly, she could hear again. "Cover yourself, you fool!" the queen bellowed.

And then Jill heard them. Waves of laughter crashed around her. She turned and began running, trying to cover herself. The faces around her were wild, howling. Their eyes were wide like moons, the makeup they wore cracked like caverns. Wild, wondering, piercing laughter cascaded down upon her. She ran, ran, ran as fast as her bare legs could carry her.

Suddenly a hand shot out from the crowd and caught her by the arm.

She turned to look. It was a beggar. His back was bent and his beard was long and scraggly. He said, "It's cold out here, Princess. Would you like a blanket?" And he handed her a rough, woolen blanket. Then he smiled. Jill covered herself with it and then sprinted back to the castle, her clay-red shoes clicking on the cobblestones, her red hair ribbons waving in the wind, her naked body running past the lines and lines of howling, laughing, weeping people.

Wow. That was unpleasant.

I am really sorry I had to tell you about that. I, who have heard this story a number of times now, am upset just retelling it. You, dear reader, must feel positively ill.

Anyway, before we conclude this story (it's not quite done!), you have a question. I know you do, because when I first heard this, the true version of this famous tale, I had the same one. It is a practical question. A small detail. And while the adults are thinking, "It's not important enough to ask," the children are demanding an answer immediately. As well they should.

The question is this: *Why couldn't Jill wear any underclothes?*

Yes! Excellent question. Exactly the right question to be asking.

The answer?

I have no idea.

Really. No clue. Because the merchant wanted to humiliate her even more? Or because he was trying to teach her a lesson? Maybe.

Or maybe it had something to do with being totally naked before all the world.

But don't listen to me. I just made that up. Make up your own explanation.

ADAM GIDWITZ

It had been many, many years since a human had entered the clearing with the well. But one cold, sunny day in spring, when the buds were tiny green pillows for the heads of silkworms and the musty perfume of thaw rose like a memory from the ground, the frog was staring up at the cerulean sky when he heard a peculiar *stomp-stomp-stomping* on the forest floor. It was followed by a sudden *whoomp*, and then a cry. Curious, he climbed the slippery stone walls to the top of his well and peered out.

Sitting on the forest floor, with matted hair and muddied clothes, was a little girl. Her face was red with anger and exertion. Her lips were all scrunched up and furious. But her eyes . . . The frog studied them. Her eyes . . . Well, her eyes looked just like the patch of sky above his well when it was its clearest, deepest blue.

The girl sat on the ground and wept. The frog felt dizzy. Was this a memory, come to life? But the longer he stared at the girl, the more certain he became that it was not. She had the same eyes, yes. But the hair was darker, curlier. Her face was not so perfect. Not nearly so perfect. And the way she cried. It was more genuine. More human.

Also, she was completely naked, save for a ratty brown blanket that she had wrapped around her body.

Should he? After twenty years? He'd lost his leg, and his heart, the last time . . .

And yet . . .

The frog took a deep breath, cleared his throat, and said, "Please, dear girl, let me help you."

The girl's head shot straight up. "Who said that?"

The frog gave her his most sympathetic froggy smile. "I did."

The girl started like she was having a heart attack.

"Yes," the frog added. "I can talk."

Another heart attack.

Then the frog said, "Can you?"

And then the girl laughed. She sniffed, wiped her nose, and nodded. "I'm Jill," she said.

"I'm Frog."

The girl laughed and sniffed again. "That's your name?" The frog shrugged. She smiled and wiped her nose on her arm.

"Can I help?" the frog asked.

Jill shrugged. "I'm running away."

"Oh . . ." said the frog. And then he had the greatest idea of his long and so far very unpleasant life. He said, "Take me with you."

"What?" exclaimed the little girl.

"Take me with you," repeated the frog. "I hate it here. I hate my well. It's wet, and mossy, and dirty, and very very very very very very very smelly."

She cocked her head at him, thinking.

"Also," he added, "there are salamanders."

"Salamanders?"

"They're terrible. Trust me."

Little Jill couldn't help but grin at the frog. She noticed that he had only three legs. The trees in the wind sounded like waves above their heads. At last, she said, "Okay."

"Okay!" cried the frog. "Where to?"

Jill thought for a minute. And then she said, "To my cousin's house."

"Excellent," said the frog. And then he said, "But do you think you should put some clothes on first?"

CHAPTER THREE

Jack and Jill
and
the Beanstalk

M arie had a little lamb, little lamb, little lamb.

Marie had a little lamb whose fleece was black as coal.

"Stop following me!" shouted Marie.

Everywhere that Marie went, Marie went, Marie went,

Everywhere that Marie went the lamb was sure to go.

"Get away from me!"

It made the children laugh and play, laugh and play, laugh and play,

It made the children laugh and play to see the lamb follow.

"Nobody wants you here!"

In a little village on the outskirts of the kingdom of Märchen, the boys had invented this song. They sang it every time they saw the little lamb. And every time they sang it, everyone would laugh.

Everyone, that is, except a little boy named Jack.

Jack, you see, was the lamb.

Once upon a time, many years before, a prince left the Castle Märchen, left his kind father the king and his bratty little sister the princess, and went out to live among the poor folk.

He did not want to live a soft life, with servants and bedspreads and tiny spoons for tea. He wanted to live a vigorous life, a hard life: to milk his own cows, chop his own wood, buy and sell like a peasant-man does. And so he did. And he lived like that for many years, until his hands grew hard as his life.

He married a fine woman, and she had a child—with big dark eyes and curly hair as black as coal. But then the woman passed away, and the man was left all alone with the little boy. He tried to raise that boy with all the vigor and hardship that a peasant's life required.

He tried, and tried, and tried, but it didn't quite work.

The boy, you see, was a dreamer.

"Where are the chickens?" his father bellowed one day. "Where are all the chickens?"

"I wanted to see them fly, Papa!" the little boy said. "But

they don't fly too good. And then a fox ate them, 'cause he was hungry." The boy smiled up at his big, strong father. His father felt little veins popping all over his forehead.

Another time, the boy put on his father's finest clothes and went swimming in the lake. Without knowing how to swim. The boy, luckily, was saved. The clothes, on the other hand, were not.

Yet another time, the boy invented a song. It went, "Jack be nimble, Jack be quick, Jack jump over the candlestick." Because the boy's name was Jack. Then he actually tried to jump over a candlestick. He knocked it over. The house burned down. Completely.

As the years went by, Jack remained a dreamer. But he became something else, too. He became a follower.

A few years after the candlestick incident, the little boy walked into his (new) house weeping. "Jack!" his father cried, "Jack! What's happened?" Jack's eyes were red and swollen, and his cheeks and arms and neck and ears were all red and bumpy and swollen, too. Jack, still crying, told his father that the boys from the village had given him a plant that would make him strong as an ox and brave as a lion. All he had to do was rub it all over himself. So he did. But it hurt and itched and he didn't want to be strong as an ox and brave as a lion if it hurt this much. Jack's father put Jack in a tub of ice water. "Before you rub a plant all over yourself, boy," his father told him, "make sure it isn't poison ivy."

It was after this incident that the famous song was invented:

Marie had a little lamb, little lamb, little lamb.

Marie had a little lamb whose fleece was black as coal.

"Stop following me!" shouted Marie.

Everywhere that Marie went, Marie went, Marie went,

Everywhere that Marie went the lamb was sure to go.

"Get away from me!"

It made the children laugh and play, laugh and play, laugh and play,

It made the children laugh and play to see the lamb follow.

"Nobody wants you here!"

Marie was a tall boy, with a sharp face and bright eyes, and he was the bravest, strongest, funniest boy in the village. If Jack could have been anyone in the world, he would not have been king of the kingdom of Märchen. He would have been king of the boys in the village. He would have been Marie.

Wait, you're telling me that "Marie" is a *boy*?

Yes. You see, in German countries, like the kingdom of Märchen was, boys are often given two names. And sometimes, the second name is Marie, or Maria. There is a famous poet named Rainer Maria Rilke. He is a boy. Well, he was a boy. Now he is dead.

Anyway, yes, I'm telling you that "Marie" is a boy.

One day, Jack's father called Jack to his side. "Do you know what tomorrow is?"

Jack nodded. "My birthday."

His father asked, "Would you like your gift now?"

Jack clapped his hands and jumped into his father's lap. But his father gently pushed him away. "Boy," he said, "it's going to be your birthday. I think it's time you started acting like a man."

Jack nodded and slowly crawled down off his father's lap.

"Not just a man, Jack. I think it's time you started acting like your own man. Taking more responsibility. And not following those boys around so much."

"I don't follow them around," said Jack. "They're my friends."

Jack's father sighed. "Anyway, money is tight. Perhaps you've noticed. You see, the cow—"

"Milky!" said Jack.

"Yes, you call her Milky," his father conceded. "Money is

tight because the cow is not giving milk anymore. We have to sell her."

"No!" cried Jack.

"And I've decided that your birthday present is the opportunity to be your own man: to take her to market all by yourself, and to sell the cow."

"I don't want to sell Milky!"

Jack's father's face grew dark. "You'll sell her," Jack's father said, "for no less than five gold pieces. You'll do it all by yourself. It'll prove that you're a man—your own man."

Jack clenched his jaw. *I'll be my own man,* he thought.

"Happy birthday," said his father.

The sun was just beginning to filter through the black pines and a rooster was crowing his head off on a nearby farm and the ragwort and the heather were rustling against each other in the wind when Jack led Milky off of his father's land and onto the road. He was taking Milky to market all by himself.

Jack and the cow walked and walked and walked and walked and walked. Milky lowed from time to time, which made Jack sad, but he just kept telling himself, "Today you become your own man. Happy birthday. Today you become your own man. Happy birthday. Today you become your own man . . ."

ADAM GIDWITZ

As Jack got closer to town, he saw many people on the road: a woman with geese all around her, honking and flapping; a man with a crooked back carrying broomsticks as crooked as he was; a tanner with stiff brown hides clacking with each step.

As the tanner passed by, he eyed Milky. He slowed his pace. He nodded at Jack.

Little Jack saw what he was carrying and jerked his head away.

Those were *cow skins.*

The tanner shrugged and walked on ahead.

Jack kept moving toward the market. After a while, he heard a strange sound behind him. It was like a rattling and a clunking and a shouting all at once. It was coming from down the road. Jack turned and looked.

He could only see a cloud of dust. But he could hear the shouting more clearly now:

"Potions, elixirs, snake oil, gin!

Tell me what ails you and give me a min . . . ute."

And then, out of the cloud of dust, emerged a broken-down cart with faded banners and rattling glass bottles on a hundred tiny shelves.

"Potions, elixirs, snake oil, gin!

Tell me what ails you and give me a min . . . ute."

Jack turned and stared at the wreck of a cart. In the driver's seat sat a greasy man with a long black ponytail. He wore a flowing, floral shirt, faded from the sun and the dust of the road. His face was round like a baby's, and his eyes were pale blue.

"Potions, elixirs, snake oil, gin!

Tell me what qils you and give me a min . . . ute."

He's not very good at rhyming, thought Jack.

And then, Jack saw, behind the cart, a group of boys from the village, pointing and laughing. They chanted, *"Potions! elixirs! snake oil! piss!*

Trade with this nut and your money you'll miss!"

Jack thought, *That's better.*

And then Jack saw who led the band of chanting, taunting children. Marie.

"Potions! elixirs! snake oil! piss!

Trade with this nut and your money you'll miss!"

The boys laughed and laughed, and Marie threw his head back and shouted it at the top of his lungs. The man in the cart didn't seem to notice.

The hulking, jerking cart pulled up beside Jack and Milky, and the man leaned out. He smiled at Jack. He was missing many teeth. "You're not selling that cow, are you?"

Jack shook his head no.

But the man grinned. "How much are you asking?"

The boys stopped chanting. Jack could feel Marie's gaze on him.

Be your own man, Jack thought. And then he said, "Five gold."

The boys began to laugh. "For that sack o' bones?" Marie bellowed.

The ponytailed man jumped down from his cart. He slapped Milky's side. "She give milk anymore?"

"No," said Jack. And then he thought, *I probably should have said yes.*

"Hmm. No milk. Scrawny as an old broom. And a hide like this wouldn't go for half a piece." He grinned at little Jack. "Tell you what I'll do. Nobody at market'll pay a penny for this cow. She'll cost more to feed than she'll ever pay out; that's why you're selling her, I reckon." The man looked knowingly at Jack.

Jack shrugged.

"Thought so," leered the man with his oily, gap-toothed smile. "So I'll give you a swap instead. It's a good swap."

Jack held on to Milky's neck and narrowed his eyes. Marie and the other children gathered closer, grinning at one another.

The man announced, "I'll swap my finest magic bean for this poor beast."

There was silence on the long, dusty road.

Then someone suppressed a snicker.

The man leaned in close to Jack and said, "I tell ya, this

bean will produce a beanstalk that'll grow straight to the sky. All you've got to do is plant it and tend it."

One of the village boys laughed out loud.

Jack was about to tell the man no—and then Marie said, "That's not a bad deal."

Jack swiveled his head at him.

The other boys stared, too.

"No," said Marie. "Really. Most of what he sells is junk. But those beans . . . Those are something."

Jack felt suddenly confused. He looked back at the man. In his dirt-encrusted hand sat a single white bean.

"It looks like a regular bean," said Jack.

Marie laughed. "It takes a real man to tend a bean like that." He turned to the salesman. "To the sky, you said?"

The man said, "That's right."

Jack asked Marie, "You think I should buy it?"

"I don't know if you can handle it," Marie replied.

"Oh, I can."

"I'd be impressed. But I doubt it."

Jack passed Milky's rope to the salesman. Then he held out his hand. The man closed the bean within it. He smiled with his round baby face and winked one pale eye at Jack. Then he hopped up on his cart, switched his horse, and rattled on into town, with Milky trailing behind.

Jack watched them go. Then he turned, beaming, back to Marie.

Marie smiled at him—and then let loose a roar of laughter.

Jack's own smile faded.

The other boys joined Marie in his hysterics. They were slapping their knees, laughing so hard they wanted to cry.

They were not the only ones who, all of a sudden, wanted to cry.

The village boys had decided to follow Jack, instead of the man with the cart. "*Jack took a cow to the market fair . . .*" they chanted.

Jack's face was hard and set as he walked toward home. Dusty tear-trails streaked both cheeks.

"*Jack took a cow to the market fair,*
Met him a swindler on the way there!"

He had chased down the man on the cart and asked him to trade back. The man had laughed at him at first. Then he had hit him with his horse switch.

"*Jack took a cow to the market fair,*
Met him a swindler on the way there!
Dumbest boy you've ever seen,
gave his cow up for a bean!"

Jack glanced over his shoulder. Marie led the other children in the chant, waving his fingers back and forth to keep time. Jack wiped his eyes with his sleeve and hurried home.

Jack's father did not listen to his story. He took one look at the bean in the little boy's hand, shouted at the top of his lungs a word that I cannot print here, and then flung the bean straight out the window. Jack went scurrying after it.

He crawled around on his hands and knees in the yard, his eyes brimming with tears.

Inside the house, his father banged doors and cabinets and occasionally shouted that word that I cannot print.

As the sun was dipping below the horizon, Jack finally found the bean. He sat by it and watched the sky light up a hundred colors. Purples and reds and oranges that had no names, as far as Jack knew. He felt as if he were burning in them. He could barely breathe. Every time his father slammed another door, he shuddered.

Happy birthday, he thought. *Today you could have become your own man.*

And then, at the edge of his father's property, Jack saw a small form crest the hill. It came toward him slowly, shufflingly. Jack watched it approach. It seemed to be a lump of brown, with two dirty human feet sticking out the bottom. It waddled right up to where Jack was sitting.

"Hello," said Jack. "What are you?"

"Your cousin," said the lump. "Dummy."

And the lump sat down on the grass beside Jack. It began to molt. The brown fell back from its head. The brown was actually just a filthy blanket, Jack could see now. Jill, also filthy (but, I should add, now wearing clothing), had been hiding under it. She smiled at him wanly.

"I had a bad day," she said.

Jack smiled in a scrunched up way. "Me too," he said. "It was my birthday."

"It was my mom's half birthday."

"I got in trouble. Really bad."

"Me too."

"What'd you do?"

"I went out in front of the whole kingdom naked."

Jack tried to stifle a laugh.

"Hey!" Jill said.

"Why did you do that?"

Jill shrugged. Then she said, "What'd *you* do?"

"I traded Milky for a bean."

Jill laughed out loud.

"The bean's magic," Jack insisted. "Wanna see?" He held it up. The moon illuminated it. It did look magic.

"It isn't magic," said Jill.

Jack looked at it. "No," he said. "I guess not." Suddenly, inside the house, Jack's father slammed something and again shouted that word I'm still not printing. Jill put her arm around Jack's shoulders. He returned the favor.

Besides being cousins, you see, Jack and Jill were best friends. Whenever one visited the other, they played imaginary games and told each other stories and made up stupid jokes together. And, every once in a while, when they really needed it, they put an arm around the other's shoulders.

"Oh, I want to introduce you to someone," said Jill.

She reached into her brown blanket and produced a frog.

"Ooh!" cried Jack. "A big fat frog!" And he grabbed the frog and held him up.

Jill tried to stop him, but Jack was too excited. "He's big and he's fat and he only has three legs!"

Then Jill said, "Jack, I think he's peeing on you."

Jack shouted and dropped the frog. Jill looked down at the plump little amphibian. "I'm sorry, Frog," she said.

"It's okay," he replied. "Boys will be boys."

Jack stared at the frog, then at Jill, then back at the frog. "Did he talk?" said Jack. Then he said, "And did you just apologize to *him*? He peed on me!"

"Yes," said Jill. "You shouldn't be so rough with him."

The frog smiled up at Jill and said, very simply, "Thank you."

Jack stared at the frog and his mouth hung open. At long last, he said, "That's amazing."

"See?" Jill said to the frog, "I told you he'd like you."

"In that case," said the frog, "Jack, I am sorry for peeing on you. We frogs don't have many defenses, you know."

Jack laughed and smiled kind of sideways. "That's okay," he said. "Little boys don't either."

And just like that, the three of them became fast friends.

And had the day ended there, it would have been a very eventful day indeed.

But it did not end there.

If it had, much suffering, much bloodshed, many tears would have been avoided.

In fact, if you're the kind of person who does not like to read about suffering and bloodshed and tears, why don't you just pretend that the day did end there, and close the book right now?

On the other hand, if you're the kind of person who does like reading about suffering, and bloodshed, and tears . . . well, may I politely ask, "What is wrong with you?"

Just then, at the edge of Jack's father's land, there was a rustling in the trees. Jack and Jill and the frog turned toward the sound, and then, in unison, they all shivered.

Standing at the edge of the property was a tiny woman, no taller than a child. Her posture was hunched, and her hair was wispy white. But her face was smooth as a baby's, and her pale blue eyes shone through the murky dusk. As she walked toward the children (and the frog), both Jack and Jill had the uncanny sensation of recognizing her. Though neither could quite place where from.

The frog whispered, "There's a creepy old lady walking toward us." He burrowed down into Jill's blanket.

When the old woman stood right beside them, she still had not said a word. There was a sudden wind, and her thin cloak fluttered. Jack realized how dark it had become. Jill felt cold.

The frog whispered, "Now there's a creepy old lady standing right next to us."

And then, the creepy old lady spoke.

"Had a bad day?" she asked. Her voice did not match her body. It was high and light and lilting, almost like a child's.

Jack and Jill stared at her, silent, mesmerized.

ADAM GIDWITZ

The frog whispered, "Now there's a creepy old lady talking to you."

Jack looked up into the strange, childlike face. "Who are you?"

"We have many names," said the old woman. The wind blew harder.

"We?"

"And we know many things. Especially about the children 'round here. You might say it's our job."

"Who's job?" said Jack.

The old woman brought her face right down beside the children's. Her pale blue eyes sparkled. "Ours," she said.

And then she said, "We'd like to do something for you."

Jill asked, "What?"

"We'd like to change your very lives."

The frog whispered, "Now there's a creepy old lady scaring the bejeezus out of me."

But Jack said, "You wanna change our lives?"

"Yes, Jack. What if everyone liked you and admired you? Especially that tall boy. What's his name?"

"Marie," Jack replied.

"Yes. Marie would admire you. And, better yet, he would like you. He, and the whole world, would really, truly like you."

There was a pause. Crickets sang through the darkness. Finally, Jack said, "You can do that?"

"Surely can," replied the old woman.

Jill squinted her eyes uncertainly.

"And you, dearie," the old woman smiled at her. "How about we make you into the most beautiful girl in the kingdom? Would that please you?"

Jill caught her breath.

"Her? Beautiful? Not possible," said Jack. Jill hit him.

The old woman chuckled. The darkness was becoming heavier, but her pale eyes shone all the more brightly.

Jill looked from Jack to the old woman. At last, the little girl said, "You can't really . . ."

"But I can, my dear. If you wish it. Do you?"

Jill stole another glance at Jack, and then she nodded fiercely. Even after the silk, and the procession, she wished for this. More than anything.

"Good," said the old woman. "You won't be sorry. Now, before we grant you these gifts, before we change your very lives, you've got to agree to do something for us in return. Nothing too onerous. A small favor. Just so we're even."

At this moment, under the spell of the old woman's words, Jack and Jill would have agreed to anything.

"We just need you to run and fetch us a glass."

"A glass?" asked Jill.

"That's easy," replied Jack. "Where is it?"

"Well," said the old woman. "It's lost. It's been lost for a little while now. But if you can find it, Jack, we will make you admired, and Jill, we will make you the beauty of the kingdom."

"You swear?" Jack asked.

The old woman's grin stretched across her wide, smooth face. "I swear on my very life," she said. "Now will you swear on your very lives to get us this glass?"

"Okay," said Jack.

The old woman looked at Jill. "And you?"

"Don't do it!" the frog hissed from deep inside the blanket.

Jill hesitated.

The old woman, in a voice as low as the wind, said, "If you swear to get that glass, I will swear to make you as beautiful as you have ever dreamed of being."

And then Jill said, "Okay."

The woman turned her pale, glowing eyes on Jack. "Now, my boy, will you give me that bean?"

"How did you know about . . . ?" Jack stammered.

The woman smiled and held out her hand. Jack, watching

her carefully, placed the bean in her wrinkled palm. The bean glowed in the bone-white light of the moon.

"Give me your thumbs," said the old woman. Jack and Jill stuck out their thumbs. The old woman plucked one of her thin, silvery hairs from her head. Then she took the end of her hair and poked Jill's thumb with it. Jill winced. A bead of blood appeared. The old woman did the same to Jack. Then to herself.

Then she scooped a handful of earth from the ground with long, hard fingernails, and placed the white bean, still shimmering by the light of the moon, in the earth. She held her thumb over the bean. She motioned for the two children to do the same. They did.

"I swear on my life," she said.

"I swear on my life," said Jack.

"I swear on my life," said Jill.

Three drops of blood spattered the white bean. Then the old woman covered the bean again with black soil.

"As soon as I'm gone," she said, "this beanstalk will grow to the sky."

"What?" said Jack.

"And when it does," the old woman smiled, "you must climb it."

"Why?" Jill objected.

"To find the glass!"

"Your cup is in the sky?" said Jack.

"It's not a cup," the old woman corrected him. "It's a glass. A looking glass. A mirror. In fact, it is called the Seeing Glass, and it is very old, and very important. In fact, it might be the most important and the most powerful looking glass in the history of the world."

Jack and Jill stared at the old lady like maybe she was a little bit insane.

Then Jill asked, "And it's in the sky?"

The old woman, to the children's great surprise, laughed. "I don't know! It has been lost for a thousand years!"

"What?" cried Jack. "So what if we can't find it?"

"You swore on your *life*," said the old woman. "If you can't find it, you die."

"What?" cried Jack again.

"What?" cried Jill.

"What?" cried the frog from inside Jill's blanket.

"What do you think *swearing on your life* means?" the old woman exclaimed. "Silly gooses." She smiled at them sweetly. "Get the Seeing Glass, or you will die. And now, good-bye!"

And without another word, the old woman made a movement toward the trees—and was gone.

The frog poked his head out of Jill's blanket and looked up at the children.

"That," he said, "was stupid."

CHAPTER FOUR

The
Giant Killer

Once upon a time, there was a beanstalk.

It started as a tiny shoot, peering up from the black soil where the bean had been planted, tender and green in the bright moonlight. Next it was a plant, small but sturdy. Then it was the size of a young tree.

All in a matter of seconds.

Soon, the beanstalk was as thick and as tall as an oak. And still it grew and grew and grew. Thick branches began to shoot out from its trunk, one every few feet, twisting upward around the great green stalk.

A little boy named Jack looked at a little girl named Jill.

"Don't do it," warned a three-legged frog named Frog. "Don't even think about it."

THE GIANT KILLER   ·

Jack took hold of a thick branch in his hands. He pulled himself onto the stalk. The branch held his weight easily. Above their heads, the beanstalk climbed and climbed and climbed, far out of sight.

"Come on," Jack said. "Let's go find that crazy old lady's glass."

"Care—ful . . . care—ful . . . careful . . . careful . . . careful, careful . . . careful careful . . . carefulcarefulcarefulcareful . . . WATCH OUT!"

Jill grabbed hold of the sprout just above her head and pulled herself up. The frog clutched desperately at the brown blanket with his toes, staring down at the tiny dot that used to look like Jack's house. The sun was just rising, slanting its yellow rays over the misty landscape below. Jill reached out her hand for the next sprout.

"Care—ful . . . care—ful . . . careful . . . careful . . . careful, careful . . . careful careful . . . carefulcarefulcarefulcareful . . . WATCH OUT!"

Jill pulled them up to the next sprout and turned to the frog. Her words were very clipped when she said, "If you don't shut up, I will drop you."

"Right," said the frog. "Sorry," said the frog. "Okay," said the frog. He tried breathing.

"Why don't you look up?" Jill suggested. "Instead of down?"

"Up? Up! Yes," said the frog. "Look up." He looked up. Then he glanced back down at the green fields, the little house, the tiny specks of cattle in the distance. "Care—ful . . . care—ful . . ." Jill gritted her teeth and concentrated on not hurling the frog to his death.

Jack was sweating, though the air was much colder up here than it had been on the ground. He looked down at Jill, and then way, way below her, to the buildings of his village. They looked tiny. So tiny. He swept his eyes out across the miniature landscape. The castle was off in the distance, tiny turrets rising like a gingerbread fort. There were swaths of mottled woods shrouded in mist, with shining rivers winding through them. He took a deep breath.

He had been right. The bean was magic. The boys had been wrong to laugh. Marie had been wrong. Jack turned and gazed into the belly of white clouds overhead.

"Where does this end?" Jill called from below.

"Are you tired?" Jack called back.

"Tired of this frog having a heart attack every time I reach for the next branch."

"Carefulcarefulcarefulcareful . . ."

Jack pointed at the clouds. "I don't know. Up there?" Jill nodded.

The thick cloud cover seemed to grow bigger and bigger above them as they climbed. Jack approached the belly of the sky, and wisps of water blanketed his face, leaving trails of dew on his cheeks and neck.

Water vapor began to clog their lungs. Jack felt like he was choking. Jill took heaving breaths. A few more feet, and they could see nothing. Gray, gray all around them, as if this part of the world had no color at all, and only a faint wetness and a cutting coldness and a swaying back and forth, back and forth.

"I can't see!" the frog cried. "I can't see and it's cold and it's wet and I can't see! I can't see and I don't want to DIE!"

Jill's teeth were chattering. "Frog," she said, "be quiet. Please."

"We're going to die, we're going to die, weregoingtodiewere-goingto . . ." the frog began repeating.

The gray around them was becoming less gray and more white. The cold was not so cold, the wet not so wet. Up, and up, and suddenly Jack felt an unexpected warmth on his face, as if he were getting close to the stove in his kitchen. The gray was now all white, and the white was becoming wispier and wispier.

And then Jack's head emerged from the clouds.

He gasped.

Jack did not blink as he climbed up to the next branch,

nor as he reached his arm out onto the blanket of clouds that surrounded him, nor even as he found that the clouds *held him up*. He did not blink once. He just stared.

Behind him, Jill pulled herself upwards, her arms shaking with strain, the sweat pouring down her face. She gave one last heave, and then she was above the cloud level.

She saw Jack, standing on the clouds. And then she saw what he was staring at.

"*Oh* . . ." she said.

Stretching out far, far into the distance was a line of towering white cliffs, undulating in and out before an endless expanse of the purest, deepest blue she could ever have imagined. The white cliffs, a thousand feet high if they were an inch, were topped with green tufts of high grass. Below the cliffs, between them and the pure blue sky, ran a long, smooth cloud beach, against which the blue of the sky gently broke like waves.

Jill gazed down the perfect white sky beach. She felt dizzy. It went on, quite literally, forever.

Jack, Jill, and the frog knelt among the clouds. They had walked for an hour down the strand of sky, marveling at the strangeness of it. But now they had stopped, for they had come upon something even stranger.

Just ahead, enormous men were punching each other, repeatedly, in the face.

"What are they doing?" Jill whispered.

A great, fat, bearded man clenched his fist, wound up, and knocked the teeth out of another great, fat, bearded man's mouth.

The great, fat, bearded man who had had his teeth punched out staggered around for a few moments, wiped the blood from his face, clenched his fist, wound up, and returned the favor.

This continued for a good many minutes. The children watched in horror.

"They look huge . . ." Jack whispered in awe.

"Giant . . ." Jill agreed.

"Not giant," whispered the frog. "*Giants*. Those are *giants*."

Neither child asked how the frog knew this, for as soon as he had said it, they knew it was true.

"I'll go talk to them," whispered Jack.

"WHAT?" cried the frog.

"*What?*" hissed Jill, not quite as loudly.

"Maybe they want to be my friend," Jack murmured.

Jill and the frog looked at Jack like he was crazy. They were

ADAM GIDWITZ

just about to tell him so, in fact, when he stood up and started for the giants.

"Jack!" Jill spat. "Stop!"

"Come back!" cried the frog.

But Jack was already walking toward the giants as if in a trance.

He had not gotten more than a few paces closer, though, when the giants suddenly wiped their bloody faces on their sleeves, turned, and trooped up a tall, thin, white staircase that led directly into a hole in the face of the cliffs. In a matter of moments, they were gone.

Jack hurried forward. Jill, reluctantly, picked up the frog and followed him.

Little Jack found himself at the base of the tall, narrow staircase that led into the cliff. He could see, at the top, a round door. Above the door ran gold lettering which read, THE CAVE OF HEROES. Before the door stood a tall, thin giant with a gaunt face and a long beard and a shining shirt of mail.

Jack gazed up at him. "Hello?" he called.

The tall, thin giant did not stir.

"Can I come up?" Jack called again.

Jill arrived at his side. *"Jack!"* she hissed. *"What are you doing?"*

But Jack was staring, fixedly, up the narrow staircase.

Jack stepped onto the first stair. The sky suddenly shook with the booming voice of the gaunt giant.

> *To enter here ye must be brave,*
> *and do what no man dare:*
> *Enter into our killing cave*
> *And face to face encounter fear.*

Little Jack nodded his head. "I'm brave!" he called up to the giant.

Jill said, "Jack! Be quiet!"

But Jack took another step up the stairs.

In response, the giant guard boomed out:

> *A band for heroes only—*
> *But join us, brave one! Try!*
> *Many before have tried to, too,*
> *And one by one each one has died.*

"I can do it," answered Jack.

"ARE YOU CRAZY?" the frog shouted. He looked to Jill. "Does your cousin have a problem or something?"

Jack took another step up the stairs.

ADAM GIDWITZ

Again, the guard bellowed to the sky:

Who shall submit his life to us?
Who shall sever his life's left hand?
Who shall place his final trust
In our unbreakable band?

"I will!" cried Jack.

"What are you doing?" Jill exclaimed, grabbing him by the sleeve. But Jack jerked his arm away and took another step up the stairs. And then another. And then another. Up, and up, and up, until he was standing directly in front of the giant. Jack came up to the middle of his thigh.

"What is he thinking?" whispered the frog, staring in abject terror.

Jill could only shake her head.

Do you have any idea what Jack is thinking right now?

No?

Me neither.

But of course, when I was Jack's age and saw people I took for giants, I never understood half the things I did either.

Suddenly, the gaunt giant guard seemed to notice Jack. He bellowed, "Who volunteers to taste fear and feel death?"

"I do," Jack replied, in his bravest voice. "Me. Jack."

Jill and the frog could only watch in horror.

"Jack, will you subject yourself to fear?"

Jack swallowed hard. "Yes," he said.

"Will you enter the band and never flee, even to the point of death?"

Jack inhaled swiftly. Jill stared.

Jack gazed at the giant's long face, his gray beard, his dead eyes.

Please, Jill thought. *Don't.*

"I will," said Jack.

"Then enter," said the guard. And he turned and led Jack into the towering white cliff.

Jack stood in a great hall. It stank of the sweat of enormous men. The walls were hung with tapestries that showed giants slaying dragons and giants destroying cities and giants making off with damsels in distress. In the center of the hall stood a huge round table. Seated at the table were two dozen giants.

"Well, what have we here?" one of the giants bellowed, rising to his feet. He wore a thin golden crown on his enormous, shaggy head. He had a long brown beard, tiny teeth in blue gums (some of which, Jack could tell, had recently been knocked out), and small, blinking eyes. He, and all the other giants seated around the table, peered curiously at little Jack.

"The boy, Jack the Small, has asked to join the band," announced the gaunt giant guard.

"Wonderful!" bellowed the one who wore the crown. "And that one?" he asked, and he waved fingers as thick as sausages at the door. Jack spun around. Standing at the top of the stairs, panting and staring, was Jill.

"It followed Jack the Small up the stairs," said the guard.

"That's Jill," said Jack. "My cousin." He smiled at her.

Jill thought, *I'm going to kill him.*

"Wonderful!" the crowned giant bellowed ecstatically. (Giants are always bellowing; sometimes they do it ecstatically and other times darkly and other times imperiously; it's just very hard not to bellow when you're a giant. You understand.) All the other giants beat the wooden table with their powerful fists. "Be welcome! I am King Aitheantas. And these are the giants of the Cave of Heroes." Then he pointed his huge sausage fingers at each one and named them. Jack didn't catch many of the names.

The guard was called Meas. There was an enormously fat one called Brod, whose stomach tumbled out over his belt in giggling lobes. And there was a skinny, young-looking one with big front teeth, whom King Aitheantas called Bucky. Bucky smiled at Jack. Jack returned the smile.

"Now," bellowed King Aitheantas, "you wonder what giants such as we might want with such a pygmy as thee?"

In fact, Jack had not wondered. But Jill said, "Yes."

The king announced, "We do not judge courage by size, do we?"

"No!" bellowed the giants. Jack grinned. Bucky flashed him a thumbs-up.

Yes, "thumbs-up" existed Once upon a time. Nowadays it means, "Good job," or, "You're okay with me." Back then, it generally meant, "My friends aren't going to kill you."

"But we must know," continued King Aitheantas, "if you are brave. You must pass harrowing tests if we are to let you join the band."

Jack said, "I will pass them."

"What happens if he doesn't?" Jill demanded.

King Aitheantas raised his eyebrows at Meas, the guard. Meas bellowed imperiously, "He dies. And so do you. The secrets of the band shall not be revealed to the world!"

Inside Jill's blanket, the frog fainted.

"First test, boulder throwing!" bellowed King Aitheantas.

"Huzzah!" bellowed the rest of the giants.

Meas left the hall to get the boulders.

The giants stood up from the great table and came and crowded around Jack, greeting him warmly. They shook his hand and slapped him on the back and welcomed him to the band.

"He's not a member yet!" Aitheantas reminded them.

"A formality! A formality!" one of them bellowed with a smile, pounding Jack on the back until he fell over.

The giants' hair was long and tangled, and some wore beards or great mustaches, while others were clean shaven. All had big rough noses and lips, and small, squinty eyes. They blinked a lot, as if their eyesight were poor.

Brod, the fat one, shouted, "Show us a muscle!" Jack obliged and Brod laughed and slapped him on the back, knocking him over again. Bucky took on a conspiratorial whisper and told Jack a joke and they both laughed, even though Jack didn't get the joke at all. Bucky shot Jack a grin and pointed at him with his finger. Jack grinned and pointed right back.

Soon, all the giants were grinning at him. "Oh, you'll be fine!" they bellowed. "Fine! Quite an impressive pygmy after all!"

And, all of a sudden, Jack didn't feel so much like a pygmy anymore. He felt, in fact, like he had always hoped to feel among Marie and the boys, and never had.

He turned and flashed a smile at Jill.

But little Jill had her arms crossed and was watching the scene from under furrowed brows. Jack thought he could see the frog, hiding under the blanket, trembling.

Then all the giants moved off to one side, and Jack saw that Meas had placed three boulders in the center of the hall. Not just any boulders. Enormous boulders. Humongous boulders. Boulders roughly the size of Jack's house, sitting there in the middle of the great hall. Jack's eyes bulged from his head.

"Not so bad, eh?" bellowed Bucky.

Jack glanced at Jill. She shook her head as if to say, "I told you."

A giant with thick, muscular arms walked up to the first boulder, bent at the knees, wedged his huge, meaty hands under the great stone, and heaved. The boulder leaped into the air, rose thirty feet above the giant's head, and then fell back to the floor with a deafening crash.

The giants roared in approval.

ADAM GIDWITZ

Another giant walked up to the second boulder. He wedged his great thick hands beneath the boulder, bent his knees, and heaved. The boulder shot forty feet into the air and then slammed back to the floor, shaking the entire hall.

The giants erupted with bellows of glee.

Jack stared at the boulders. He looked around at the giants' faces. They were grinning at him. He swallowed hard and approached the third boulder.

He bent his knees.

He pushed his hands under it as far as they would go.

He lifted.

He lifted some more.

He lifted even more than that.

The boulder, of course, did not budge. At all.

His arms and back and hands aching, Jack stepped away from the great rock and looked around.

The giants were not smiling any longer.

"Go ahead," said King Aitheantas. "Throw it in the air."

Jack's throat felt dry. "I can't," he said.

"You'd better," bellowed Aitheantas, "or your life is forfeit."

Jack winced and tried to wipe away the sweat that was pouring into his eyes. "What does 'forfeit' mean again?" he asked.

"It means you die!" cried Bucky. "Now lift it!"

Jack hurriedly stuck his hands underneath the boulder. He bent his knees. He heaved.

And heaved.

And heaved.

Nothing.

When he staggered away from the stone this time, the giants were staring at him balefully. "You said you were brave!" bellowed Aitheantas.

"I am!" cried Jack, his voice wilting in his throat. "I'm just not strong enough!"

"Courage is strength! Strength is courage! Boy, your life is ours!" Aitheantas cried.

"Wait!" shouted Jack. "Wait! Let me try again! Let me try another test!"

Aitheantas had started moving toward Jack. But the little boy's pleading cries made him pause. Slowly, he said, "Shall we let him try another test?"

The hall was deathly still. At last, Brod said, "Let him break sticks!"

"Huzzah!" bellowed the other giants.

Aitheantas nodded. "Then break sticks he shall. Meas, fetch the sticks."

Jack exhaled. *They saved me*, he thought. *I can break a few sticks.*

And he looked at Jill as if to say, "See? They're my friends after all."

Jill glowered at him and slowly shook her head from side to side.

When Jack saw the sticks, he nearly fell over. They were tree trunks. Three tree trunks. Bound together with thick, heavy rope. Meas deposited them in the middle of the chamber. Then he rolled the boulders away.

"Go ahead, boy!" bellowed Aitheantas. "Break 'em!"

Jack walked reluctantly up to the tree trunks. He gazed at them. He whispered, "Do I have to?"

"Oh, yes," said Aitheantas.

In a very small voice, Jack asked, "Can I just give up now and leave?" He sounded like he might cry.

"Oh, no," said Aitheantas. The hall was totally silent now. The giants' tiny eyes followed Jack closely.

Jack reached out his arms and tried to wrap them around the tree trunks. They barely reached halfway around. He tried to sit on the trunks. That did nothing. He got up and jumped on them. They didn't even creak.

Jack's hair was soaked with sweat, and his lips were trembling. The giants' faces were dark and terrible.

"Well," said Aitheantas, "you know the rules."

"No!" Jack whispered. "Let me live! Please!"

"Oh, we'll let you live," said Aitheantas.

"You will?"

"Yes. Until after dinner. Then we'll kill you and eat you for dessert."

"HUZZAH!" bellowed the giants.

Jack sat huddled in a corner, crying quietly. Jill's arm was around his small shoulders.

"I'm sorry," he whimpered.

"What were you thinking?" the frog hissed through Jill's blanket.

Jack buried his head deeper in his arms.

But Jill was watching the giants. Her eyes traveled to the door. It was locked and barred. She looked back at the giants, with their huge bellies, their thick faces, and their tiny, watery eyes.

They sat around their enormous table. Heaped upon it was a feast of fowls: geese and hawks, kites and eagles, merlins and jays; roasted, panfried, boiled in blood, chopped up, blackened. The smells of roasted flesh and dripping fat wafted through the hall.

The giants were just about to tuck in when Bucky said, "I am about as hungry as any giant has ever been, I reckon."

At this, Brod, the very fat giant, pushed back from the table and chuckled. "Well, Bucky, that sounds like a challenge to Brod."

And, because no giant-hero can turn down a challenge

when offered, Bucky replied, "If it's a test you want, it's a test you'll have. Can you eat more than me?"

Brod laughed and grabbed his huge stomach.

"Your belly's big," replied Bucky, "but that just means I have more room to grow!"

The other giants huzzahed the brave words and banged on the table. But King Aitheantas said, "Bucky, you're a whelp, and Brod, you're a coward to challenge such a whelp. If you can outeat me, *then* I'll be impressed."

"Or me!" shouted another giant.

"Or me!" bellowed another. Soon all the hall was a cacophony of giant voices, all crying to participate in the challenge. Meas went off to get something called the Bowl of Never Ending, for the tableful of fowl would have been no more than an appetizer to a challenge such as this.

Jill gazed at the giants howling for the commencement of the challenge. Then she took the frog out of her pocket and handed him to Jack.

"Give me your belt," she said.

"What?"

"Now."

He looked at her like she was crazy. But Jill was still staring at the giants. As he took off his belt, Jill wrapped her ratty brown blanket all the way around her, and then she took Jack's belt and cinched it so tight she could barely breathe. Jack watched her, befuddled. Jill stuck out her chin and walked to the giants' table.

"Excuse me," she announced. "Can I accept the challenge?"

All the giants turned and looked at her.

The only sound in the sudden silence was Jack whispering, "Uh . . . Jill?"

King Aitheantas's face slowly broke into a wide grin. "Well, look at that! Why didn't you say she was the brave one, Jack?" Jack's face went red.

The giants roared with approval and pulled up a chair for the little girl.

"What's she doing?" the frog hissed frantically. Jack shook his head.

"Eat till you burst," Brod said to Jill.

"Or until you do," she answered, and all the giants shouted and banged the table and pointed their thick sausage fingers approvingly at her.

"She's the courageous one!"

"She's a winner!"

"Let's see what the pygmy can do!"

Meas came back with the Bowl of Never Ending. It was an enormous wooden bowl that was never empty. Unfortunately it was always full of porridge, and the porridge generally had a sickening, burned taste, so the giants avoided eating from it when they could. But only the Bowl of Never Ending would suffice for such a challenge as this. Whoever ate the most platefuls without throwing up won. Meas heaped each plate with bird meat, until no fowl was left on the table. Then, with an enormous spoon, he poured a sickeningly large dollop of porridge on top of the fowl. The porridge steamed and stank like something burning. Brod licked his lips. Jill felt like she might gag.

What follows is the most disgusting thing I have ever heard in any tale I have ever come across.

I considered cutting it completely from this record. I feel sick just thinking about it. Writing it down for you was, shall we say, a harrowing experience.

But, as I promised to tell you the true story of Jack and Jill, I must include what follows.

You, though, have no obligation to actually *read* it.

"A *haon!*" shouted Aitheantas, and the giants all picked up their spoons. "A *dó!*" he cried, and all the giants put down their spoons and gripped the sides of their plates. "A *trí!*" he bellowed, and all the giants poured their meat and porridge straight down their gullets. They slammed their plates down, and Meas filled them all in the blink of an eye. The giants lifted their plates to their mouths and poured another helping down their throats.

Jack turned to look at Jill. She, too, had a second plateful before her. She picked it up and began pouring it over her open mouth. But, Jack noticed, most of the porridge did not go into her mouth. In fact, none of it did. She seemed to be licking it up with her tongue, but as Jack watched he saw that she was actually pushing it out onto her face. From there, it slid, hot and terrible smelling, down her neck and into the ratty brown blanket. She slammed her plate down like the rest of them and started again.

Jill poured another plateful over her face and down her shirt. Around the table, giants gobbled the revolting stuff down. Only Brod seemed to be enjoying it.

Slam! More porridge pouring down the giants' gullets, more porridge sliding down Jill's neck.

Slam! Slam! Slam! Slam! The porridge was now visibly collecting in the brown blanket, hanging over Jill's belt in what looked for all the world like a jiggling belly.

Slam! Slam! Slam! Slam! Slam! Slam!

ADAM GIDWITZ

Jill smiled as she poured more of the sickening glop over her face and down her neck. The giants, on the other hand, started to look ill.

Slam! Slam! Slam! Slam! Slam! Slam! Slam! Slam!

Twenty servings in, Bucky had begun to slow down. *Slam! Slam! Slam! Slam!* After twenty-four, he looked positively green. *Slam! Slam! Slam! Slam!* After twenty-eight, Bucky turned and threw up all over the floor. The smooth, velvety vomit spread over the flagstones. Its odor suffused the hall and made Jack gag.

"Bucky is out!" cried Meas. The other giants let out a muffled cheer and continued pouring the sludge-like porridge down their throats.

Slam! Slam! Slam! Slam! Slam! Slam! Slam! Slam! Slam! Slam! Slam! Slam!

After forty helpings, two giants turned and threw up at exactly the same time, their chunky vomit mingling on the floor. "Goleor and Barraoicht are out!" Meas bellowed.

Bucky was staring at Jill. "How is she still eating?" he asked. But no one was listening.

Slam! Slam! Slam! Slam! Slam! Slam! Slam! Slam! Slam! Slam! Slam! Slam! Slam! Slam! Slam! Slam!

Now giants were throwing up all over the place. Chunks,

globs, nuggets of bloody, fatty vomit coated the flagstones, the table legs, the giants' legs.

"Leithleach out!" Meas bellowed. "Feall out!" "Aitheantas out!" One by one, each giant erupted like a volcano of half-digested pink meat and gray porridge.

The upchuck began collecting in a large pool under the table, and then began to spread out over the floor, like some gooey, primordial lake. The giants were slouching in their chairs, covered with silky brown sludge, groaning. But Jill kept pouring the porridge over her face and letting it slide down her neck. Brod was still eating, too. But he had begun to slow.

Slam . . . Slam . . .

Slam . . .

Wobble . . .

Brod stopped with a plate full of porridge in front of him.

"Brod?" Meas asked. All the giants leaned forward and looked at the enormous slab of meat known as Brod.

"Uhhhhghhh."

"Do you give up, Brod?" Meas wanted to know.

"Uhhhhghhh," said Brod.

"Well?"

Brod threw up all over the table.

"Jill is the winner!" announced Meas.

ADAM GIDWITZ

Jill stood up triumphantly. Jack cheered his head off. The frog did little fist pumps in Jack's pocket.

The giants stared at Jill. The blanket had stretched out into the largest stomach any of them had ever seen. Even bigger than Brod's. It hung down over her belt, all wobbly and gelatinous.

And then, the silence was cut with the word "Cheat!"

Bucky was pointing at her, his face red. "She's a cheat!"

Aitheantas glared at her. "I believe she is," he said.

"She didn't eat that porridge!" said Bucky. "She couldn't have."

"I don't believe she could," said Aitheantas. Brod threw up on the table again.

"You don't believe me?" Jill cried. "You dare question me?" Her voice was fierce, frightening. "I will show you the food in my belly, if you will show me the food in yours."

"Mine's mostly on the table," said Brod.

"I challenge you all to show me the food in your bellies!" Jill bellowed.

Aitheantas rose to his feet. A cunning smile played across his lips. "If you, my little pygmy, can show us the food in your belly, we can show you the food in ours."

Jill turned to Meas. Very slowly, very clearly, she said, "Bring us knives."

I don't believe anyone is reading right now. I assume everyone has just skipped to the next chapter. I hope so.

If any of you are indeed still reading this . . . well . . . good luck to you.

Meas disappeared and returned in a moment, carrying enough long, sharp knives for every giant in the hall, and one for Jill. Jill grasped hers in her hand. "Show me your food!" she cried.

"Jill!" Jack cried. "Stop!" The frog peered out of his pocket.

Jill raised the knife above her head. Then she brought the knife down and buried it in her stomach. It entered her body just above the belt; from there she drew it up the length of her enormous belly.

The frog fainted again.

Porridge poured out all over the floor. Inside Jill's shirt was a mess of brown tatters, fleshy porridge, and bird bones. Jack stared. Between the ratty brown of the blanket and the disgusting mess of meat and bone and porridge, it looked a whole lot like human entrails.

The giants all squinted their tiny eyes at Jill and her dissected shirt.

"I can do that!" Bucky cried. And he plunged his knife into his stomach and drew it from his belt to his throat. Blood and porridge poured out onto the floor, and then Bucky fell down. Dead. His eyes were wide, and his corpse lay half submerged in vomit.

"So can I!" cried Leithleach. And he, too, gutted himself, spilling his blood and viscera and porridge, and then collapsing on top of them.

"Me too!"

"So can I!"

"That's easy!"

And one by one, each giant-hero cut himself from gullet to gizzard, and an explosion of blood and guts and partially digested meat and porridge poured all over the floor of the hall. One by one, each giant collapsed into the blood and vomit. The floor was six, now eight, now ten inches deep with blood and guts and food. Each time a giant fell, the steaming, putrid pool rippled.

Aitheantas was the last. "I'm not sure I can," he said, looking uncertainly around at the carnage.

"You have to, King," Meas said. "You accepted the challenge."

"There's no way out of it?" Aitheantas asked forlornly.

Meas shook his hoary beard. "None," he said.

Aitheantas looked balefully at Jill. Then he took a deep breath, clutched his knife tightly in his hand, and cut a long gash from below his belly button to the top of his neck. Porridge and guts and blood poured out of his enormous body, and then he tumbled like a felled tree to the floor. The pool of pink and brown muck around him rippled, and then grew still.

Jill pulled off the long, stretched, tattered, and filthy blanket to reveal her equally filthy shirt.

"Well," said Meas impassively, "that was a neat trick."

"Thanks," Jill replied.

Jack stared at the carnage around him, trying to figure out what had just happened.

"Are you going to let us go?" Jill asked the gaunt old guard.

"Certainly," he replied. He stuck out his giant, bony, sallow-skinned hand to Jill. She shook it. "I hated those brutes," he said. "They got exactly what they deserved." Then Meas shook Jack's hand, patted the frog on his little head and, wading through great lake of giant blood and vomit, showed them to the narrow staircase out of the cave.

"Wait," said Jill. "Do you have the Seeing Glass?"

Meas's dim eyes seemed to glow brighter for a moment. "Ah," he said. "Is that why you came here?"

"It was," said Jill. "Until Jack forgot."

"I didn't forget," Jack mumbled, turning red.

"It isn't here." Meas's voice replied. "But it is indeed a treasure worth seeking. The greatest power, it is said, resides in that Glass. A piece of true magic, as strong and pure as any in the world."

"Do you know where it is?" Jill asked.

"We are as high up as this earth goes, save Heaven. The Glass, last I heard, was in the deepest pit of the earth, save Hell. You might try there."

"How do we get there?" Jack asked.

Meas shrugged. "Ask the goblins."

"Goblins?"

Meas nodded his great gray head. "But be careful. Giants are brutal. Goblins are cunning. Do not trust them too far."

"How do we find them?"

"I don't know. I have never left this cave."

The children gazed up at his long, sad face. "But there's no more band, right?" Jill asked. "Can't you leave now?"

Meas sighed. "There will always be a band. As long as there are giants, there will be fools who will follow them."

Jack was about to ask what he meant, but Meas turned around and muttered, "Now where did I put that bucket?"

Jack walked quietly, sullenly, across the linen-white clouds under the towering chalky cliffs. Jill followed with the frog.

Jill and the frog talked on and on about what they had just seen and done.

"And did you see how Bucky just grabbed the knife and jammed it into his stomach?"

"And Aitheantas's face when he realized what was happening?"

"Meas was actually pretty nice!"

"I've never seen anything so disgusting in my life!"

"You were pretty great, Jill," the frog said.

"Yeah," Jack cut in, his first word since leaving the cave. "Great." He didn't sound happy at all.

Jill looked over at him. "What's with you?" the frog demanded.

"I could have done that," little Jack insisted. "I could have saved us."

Neither Jill nor the frog said anything.

"And it was so obvious what you did. I can't believe they were so dumb to fall for it!" Jack looked very angry. His dark eyebrows made a sharp downward arrow, and his cheeks were flushed.

The wind blew in off the wide blue sky. The sun was setting behind the cliffs, throwing long shadows over the beach. Somewhere far below them, they could hear the call of gulls.

"You went in there," said the frog to Jack. "It's your fault. And Jill saved us."

"You're an ugly girl and a stupid three-legged frog!" Jack shouted at them, and without warning he sprinted ahead.

"Jack! Jack!" the frog called after him.

"Let him alone," Jill said sadly.

Jack ran, and the wind blew across his face.

Why? he thought. *Why does this keep happening? The boys in the village, the giants, Aitheantas, Bucky, Marie . . . it's all the same. It will always be the same.* Hot tears of humiliation streaked down Jack's cheeks and blurred his vision. He ran, and ran, and the wind was strong, and growing stronger, and then suddenly it was very strong indeed.

Jill and the frog suddenly could not see Jack anymore. "Jack!" Jill cried. She started running after him. Suddenly, she felt the clouds under her feet fail.

Then she saw Jack. He was doing just what she was doing.

He was plummeting toward the earth.

Jill tumbled and tumbled and tumbled through the air. The frog was screaming, but Jill felt oddly calm. Then, beneath Jack,

Jill saw a smooth, green hill rising to greet them. Beside the hill was a little town, and beside that, the sea. As Jill tumbled, the hill and the town grew and grew and grew, and she thought, *That will be a nice place to land.*

Then she did land there, on top of that green hill, and it hurt very much. But she was not done tumbling. She tumbled all the way down that big green hill, until she landed in a heap at the bottom, next to Jack.

Jill sat up, laughing. The frog had gone from screaming to whooping for joy. "We're alive!" he shouted. "Thank God! We're alive!" Then he stopped. He saw Jack.

Jack was not laughing. His face was white and still, and there was blood pooling in the green grass under his head.

Jill got up, saw they were on the outskirts of the town, and ran screaming for the nearest house.

CHAPTER FIVE

Where You'll Never Cry No More

Once upon a time, in a little seaside town, a boy named Jack was put into bed in the attic room of the town's only inn. Jill sat down on the bed beside him and stared. The bandages on his head were red and soaked through, and his face was very pale.

"Will he be all right?" Jill asked quietly.

The innkeeper stood in the doorway, her hands on her hips. She answered Jill in her broad, salty accent. "I fancy he will. He just needs a bit a sleep, and some food, and he'll be right as the rain, I reckon." Her Rs were broad and rolling, like everything else about her. They made Jill feel a little seasick. Or maybe that was seeing Jack, as still and pale as death.

"Thank you," Jill said.

"You can come down when you're ready," the innkeeper said. Jill had agreed to help out around the inn—sweep the floors, do the dishes, that sort of thing—in exchange for the room and food.

Jill nodded and the innkeeper left. Jill knelt down by Jack. Gently she pulled back the covers. He did not stir.

The frog had been weeping quietly ever since he'd seen Jack there at the base of the hill. "Leave me here," he said, and Jill took him from her pocket and placed him, oh so gently, on Jack's chest. "I'll keep watch," the frog said. "You go downstairs now and earn our keep." He smiled his bravest froggy smile at Jill. Jill returned the smile sadly, stole a final glance at pale Jack, and went downstairs with a heavy heart.

That night, Jill was kept very busy in the tavern. She cleaned up spilled ale and cleared scotch whisky glasses from the rough wooden tables and brought plates of kippered herring and cracked snails in pails. It seemed that every fisherman and his wife was in the tavern that night. They stank of fish, but their smiles were broad, and their eyes twinkled kindly when Jill came by.

"Now, what have we here?" a big-bellied man said. "What's this wee lass doin' in our town?"

Jill answered their questions in a vague sort of way and tried not to drop any dishes on the floor. The work and the talk and

114

all the new people helped Jill to think just a little bit less about the pale boy with the red bandage who lay on the verge of death upstairs.

After the townspeople had all been drinking for a long while, the big-bellied man called Jill over to him. He had a shiny bald head and a big red beard. He smiled at Jill and his eyes twinkled. "You wanna hear a story, then?" His breath smelled like whisky and his clothes smelled like fish.

"Now don' scare the girl," someone shouted at him, and "girl" had too many syllables.

The red-bearded, big-bellied man laughed and looked at Jill. "I don't think ya scare easily. Do ya?" Jill set her chin and shook her head. He bellowed with laughter and said, "See!"

So he set her on a stool beside him, and the tavern quieted down, and the man began to tell his story.

"Once upon a time," he said, "there was a wee fishin' village that sat next to the wide black sea, in the shadow of some high green hills."

"They're mountains!" someone shouted.

"Me foot!" called someone else, and everybody laughed.

"In the shadow of high green *hills*," the red-bearded man repeated, smiling, and his Rs rolled like rowboats on the ocean. "And in this wee town there was a wee lass. Just about the size of ye," and he poked Jill in the chest with a thick finger. Reluctantly, Jill smiled.

"Well, this lass loved the sea," he continued. "She would go out and stare at it, drinkin' in its vastness and its darkness, as if the black waves made some kind of mirror where she could see herself. At least, that's what the villagers whispered to one another as they watched her, with the wind blowin' her hair this way and that, at the end of the rocks."

The tavern had gone silent now. Someone began to snuff out the candles, one by one, until the only light came from the flickering peat fire. The hairs on Jill's arms began to rise and stand up.

"But thas not what the lass was looking at. She weren't *lookin'* at nothin'. She were listenin'. Listenin' to the song of the mermaid."

"I knew it!" someone shouted. "The man's obsessed with the mermaid!"

"Shhhh!" hushed all the others. And the red-bearded man went on.

"The mermaid sings more beautiful than any mortal has ever heard. Her notes rise like gulls on the wind, and sink like the moon sinks into the sea. She holds 'em high, and sings 'em way down low, like the very sea itself. But no mortal can hear them save a young girl. And no young girl can ever resist their sound.

"Well, one day, the mermaid spoke to that little girl, her hair bein' blown 'round, way out on the rocks. And the mermaid asked if the little girl wouldna like to come and live with her under the sea. And the little girl said she would. Well, tha' night, as we sat here in this tavern, we looked out the window and saw a great black wave rise up out o' the sea. And that wave swallowed the wee lass whole. And we ne'er saw her again. And that's the truth."

The tavern was silent now.

At last, Jill whispered, "Is that really the truth?"

"We don't know," the innkeeper said. "We did a lose a lass in the sea years ago. But all this mermaid stuff? That's just a tale told."

"It's true enough!" the red-bearded man said. "There is a mermaid out there. I've seen her."

"Have ye heard her?" someone asked.

"No, she sings only to the little girls," said the man. "But she's out there all righ'."

"And how do you know it was she that took the girl and not jus' the sea?"

"I know," said the bearded man darkly. "I jus' know."

After that, the people of the tavern filed out into the pitch blackness, wending their way over stones and dirt to their homes that climbed the sides of the hills. Jill followed them out and watched them go. She watched the red-bearded man particularly. She saw that he lived all alone, in a small hut that stood closer to the rocks and the sea than any of the other villagers.

Jill wondered about the little girl who had disappeared. She wondered if she liked it under the sea, with the mermaids. She went up to her room, wanting to tell Jack the story. But he was still asleep. As was the frog, who was snoring ridiculously. She decided not to wake them.

The windows were like walls it was so black out. No moon, no stars, no light at all. The wind rattled the door on its hinges, and the sea spumed and tossed. Jill, lying on her little bed of straw, could hear the crash of the waves against the craggy rocks. She had never felt such a night, never known the fear and thrill of lying so close to sea and wild. Her body sang. She could not sleep.

Late, late that night, when the wind had died down and the crash of the waves on the rocks had subsided into a calm, rhythmic beat, Jill sat up in bed. Just above the sound of the waves, she heard a high note, held for an impossibly long time.

A *weather vane*, Jill thought. *It must be the creaking of a weather vane.*

The note fell—no, it swooned, as if fainting. Then it rose again, running in and out of the beating waves like a flute among a slow, funerary pulse of drums. Jill lay back down. Just a weather vane. Or hinges, creaking.

She lay in bed, listening to the long, plaintive sound. It stretched out across the darkness, and in the corners of the night it seemed to wrap into a pattern of words. *Yes,* Jill thought as she stared at the ceiling and listened. The notes had words. She sat up again and tried to hear them. She did hear them.

Come, come, where heartache's never been, the song went.
And where you're seen as you want to be seen.
Come, come, the place of shadow and green,
Where you'll never cry no more, dear lass,
Where you'll never cry no more.

Slowly, Jill got up from the bed and walked to the window. She looked out onto the empty, ghostly town. The dirt road led down to the rocks, where the water splashed black and white in spouting spumes. The sea was as dark as anything she had ever seen, but the obsidian waves shone white as they crested and caught the light of the moon now rising. Jill shivered. Again she listened to the word-like sounds.

Come, come, where heartache's never been.
And where you're seen as you want to be seen.
Come, come, the place of shadow and green,
Where you'll never cry no more, dear lass,
Where you'll never cry no more.

It was no weather vane. It was a song—sung by a voice unlike any Jill had ever heard. Like a gull rising on the wind, or the moon sinking into the sea.

She turned to see if the song had woken Jack. But he slept on, heavy and senseless to the music amid the black, still night.

Suddenly, she shook her head and laughed at herself. *It's the villagers*, she realized. *Playing a joke on me. Tomorrow they'll ask me if I heard something strange in the night*, she thought. *Just wait and see.*

She got back in bed. It was a haunting voice, whomever it belonged to. *The voice of a girl*, Jill thought. She listened to the words: *where heartache's never been; where you're seen as you want to be seen; where you'll never cry no more*. As Jill slept that night, she dreamed of such a place, a place of shadow and green.

In the morning, the innkeeper rapped loudly on the bedroom door. "Up! Work!" she shouted.

ADAM GIDWITZ

Jill sat straight up in bed. She looked over at Jack. He smiled wanly at her.

"Hi," he said weakly.

She leaped up and threw her arms around him.

"Sorry," he said. "for being so stupid, up there in the clouds."

"It's all right," Jill laughed.

"No it isn't!" said the frog.

"Wish I could help with your work," Jack said. His voice was thin and tired.

"You rest," Jill smiled. And then she said, "Did you hear music last night? Singing?" Jack shook his head. Jill shrugged. "You slept heavily."

"I didn't hear anything either," said the frog.

"You were snoring your head off," Jill replied. She went downstairs.

All day, no villager said a word about any song in the night. As the townspeople gathered for dinner and drinking that evening, Jill tried to detect hidden smiles, or signs of a communal jest. But there were none.

That night, as she lay in bed, she heard the song again. She looked over at Jack. He was sound asleep. The frog was buried under the covers, but she could make out his even breathing as well, in tiny syncopation with Jack's.

The song reverberated through the timbers of the old inn. Jill covered her head with a straw pillow and tried to ignore it.

A minute later, Jill was out of bed. She slipped silently down the creaky wooden steps of the inn, out the door, and guided her bare feet down the dirt path to the rocky shore. In front of her, the waves heaved against the crags of rock, shooting their white foam high into the black air. But off to the right, down a little ways from the village, there was a calmer spot, where the water rolled into and spiraled away from a ten-foot-wide rock harbor. Jill walked out there. Above her, the night was clear and very cold, and the stars twinkled sharply. Jill came to the little harbor. She felt faint spray on her face and smelled the heavy salt of the sea. And she heard the song.

Come, come, where heartache's never been.
And where you're seen as you want to be seen.
Come, come, the place of shadow and green,
Where you'll never cry no more, dear lass,
Where you'll never cry no more.

She sat down on the black rocks of the little harbor—it would have looked like a wide crescent bay to a toy ship—and she watched the rolling foam swirl in and away. And then, rising out of the sea, sending shivers up and down her back, green as the ocean by day and black as the ocean by night and capped by white foam and moonlight, came a mermaid.

That's right, folks. A real live mermaid.
     Don't ask me. I'm just telling it like it was.

The mermaid placed her body on a flat stone just a little way into the tiny harbor. Her body—at least, all of her body that Jill could see—was beautiful and naked. Halfway down her moonlight-hued back, green fish scales, lined with shadow, began. Her eyes were black and green with no whites at all. Her hair was the color of the night water reflecting the moon. The singing had stopped. Jill stared.

     "A beautiful, beautiful girl," the mermaid said, her eyes so wide set and luminous she looked like a creature from a dream, "You are a beautiful, beautiful girl." Jill was unable to answer her.

     "Yet you are sad," the mermaid said, and then she gasped, and her shoulders contracted as if in pain. "So sad! Beautiful girl, what could cause you such pain?"

The wind off the sea blew the spray into Jill's eyes and face, and her hair whipped around her like a rope on a sail. "How can you tell that I'm sad?" Jill asked, and she felt that she was shivering.

The mermaid looked at her with those wide, black and green eyes. "I come from a place where there was once no sadness. Now that I know sadness, I feel it too strongly to be borne. Tell me, beautiful girl, tell me: why are you so sad?"

Jill looked down. The mermaid said, "Something to do with your mother," and it was not a question. There was a pause in which only the crashing waves spoke. "Let us talk about other things," said the mermaid.

So they did. They talked about the mountains, and the stars, and the sea. And after a while, Jill began to feel better.

Jill looked up and saw the first streaks of pink in the sky out over the ocean. The mermaid felt them without seeing them. "I must go," the mermaid said. "But come tomorrow if you like. We will talk some more."

"Yes," Jill said, "I would love to come. Thank you."

The mermaid smiled. She was about to slide down the rock and back into the sea when she said, "Jill, do not tell the villagers that you spoke to me. There is one who would harm me if he could."

Jill stared at the beautiful creature. Who could ever want to harm her? She nodded. "I will not tell. I promise."

The next morning Jill slipped out of her room with no more than a syllable to Jack, and all day she was unable to keep her mind on her work. She dropped two glasses to the floor and then cut her hand as she cleaned up the shards. The innkeeper spoke to her sternly about her carelessness. Jill just wanted night to come.

At last, the villagers had gone home. Jill went to her bedroom.

"Did you break *two* glasses today?" Jack asked as she walked in. "That's what it sounded like from up here."

"I just want to go to sleep," Jill said sharply. Jack looked surprised, and then away. The frog stared at Jill.

Jill got into bed and turned her back to Jack. "How are you doing?" she asked without feeling.

"Fine," Jack said as he blew out the oil lamp by his bed. He didn't sound fine. He sounded angry. Jill didn't care.

She waited until she heard the first note of the mermaid's song, checked that Jack was indeed breathing softly and evenly, and then hurried straight down to the little harbor. As she hurried, she sang along with the mermaid:

Come, come, where heartache's never been.

And where you're seen as you want to be seen.

Come, come, the place of shadow and green,

Where you'll never cry no more, dear lass,

Where you'll never cry no more.

When the mermaid rose out of the sea and onto the rock, Jill marveled at her moonlit body, her blacks, her greens, her eyes, her hair.

"There is my beautiful friend," said the mermaid. Jill shook her head in the strong wind, but smiled anyway.

"Mermaid," Jill said, "you told me last night that you came from a place where there was once no sadness. Is there sadness there now?"

"Yes," replied the mermaid.

"But why?"

"Do you remember," the mermaid asked, "that I told you there was one who would harm me if he could?"

"Yes."

"Once upon a time," she said, "there were seven sisters who lived beneath these waves. I was the youngest. Each of my sisters was more beautiful than the last, and each more kind and more good. We would rise up on this rock and sing to the people of this village, and they loved us. Indeed, there was a little girl who loved us more than anything, and she wanted to live with us, down in the dark and green sea, where there is no sadness. You see, her mother had died of a great sickness, and she was left alone with her cruel father. When she asked if she could come to live with us instead, we told her no. A little girl, we thought, should live with her kind above the waves. But then we learned that she too was sick, and if she stayed in the village she would surely die. So we relented, and one night she joined us, and then there were eight sisters.

"But her father was furious with us. He cast a net and caught my oldest sister and cut her throat, so her blood, dark and green, flowed over her beautiful smooth skin. Some weeks later, he caught my second eldest sister in his net, and again he cut her throat and spilled her dark green blood. Again and again he caught my sisters, until at last there were only me and his daughter left, living here under the sea.

"The little girl was so sorry for what her father had done that she became sick with grief. After seven days and seven nights of pining, she died from her sadness."

The mermaid's wide-set eyes and moon-hued lips looked like they might burst with sorrow. But she said no more.

"That's terrible," Jill cried. "Oh, it's awful, it's awful!"

Suddenly, her sorrow for her own troubles seemed so small and stupid. "Let me help you!" Jill said, "Please! What can I do?"

The mermaid shook her head sadly. "What is there to be done?" she asked. "They are all dead. There is nothing to be done but weep." And Jill could see that rivers of tears had been steadily streaming down the mermaid's face for many years, and had dug shallow canyons in her cheeks.

"Who is the man? Does he still live in the village?" Jill demanded fiercely.

The mermaid nodded sadly. "I don't know who he is. I cannot see the faces of men. Just beautiful girls like you. But he still comes out some nights with his net and tries to catch me. I never know when. I believe he will not rest until I am dead. But what does it matter? My sisters, my sweet sisters, have all died already."

"He will not kill you," Jill swore, her teeth set, her hair blown back, her forehead shining high and wet with sea spray in the moonlight. "I will not let him do that."

When pink began to streak the east, Jill blew a kiss to the beautiful mermaid and went back to the tavern.

The next morning, Jack was awake before Jill. She got up, and he smiled at her.

ADAM GIDWITZ

"I'm sorry for last night," she said.

"You were tired from working all day."

"Yes," she said. "Very tired. Are you feeling better?"

"A little bit better each day," Jack replied. "But sitting here is boring."

Jill was humming a slow, sad tune when she slipped into the corridor.

As Jill scrubbed the tables in the tavern and the innkeeper shined the scotch glasses, Jill said, "Whose daughter was it that got lost in the sea?"

The tavern mistress stopped her shining and looked at Jill curiously. "Now what made ye think o' that, lass?"

Jill shrugged and went back to scrubbing. "Dunno. Just thinking."

The tavern mistress shook her head. "The man what told the story," she said. "With the red beard."

Jill nodded. "That's what I thought."

She watched him as he ate his dinner and then drank his scotch and ale. He laughed plenty and told stories and seemed to be liked by all. But there was something about him. Something sad. In the pauses between stories, or when his big-bellied laughter died away, she saw him sigh or look down at the table heavily. She didn't know why she hadn't seen it before. Once, he caught her looking at him. She smiled quickly. He broke into a broad grin. This time, when he looked away, he did not sigh.

Jill ran down to the edge of the rocks that night and told the mermaid that she knew who it was that was trying to hurt her. The mermaid nodded sullenly. "What good will that do, though?" she asked, and her lips and her face and her eyes were so sad and fine they made Jill want to weep. "He will not stop."

"I'll make him stop," Jill said. "I swear it. I swear it."

This time, as the pink began to streak the eastern sky, the mermaid blew Jill a kiss. Jill felt it on her cheek, like soft sea foam.

The next afternoon, Jill made her way down to the little hut by the sea where the red-bearded man lived. She knocked on the door. There was no answer. So she went around to a small shed that stood behind the house to look for him there. The door stood ajar. Jill looked within.

Hanging from the walls of the shed were dozens of rusty fish axes and harpoons, each covered with fish guts and algae and filth. Covered, that is, save their edges. Those shone sharp and clean.

"Hello there!"

Jill turned around to see the red-bearded man sitting on a stack of peat bricks against the wall of the house, mending a fishing net. "Why, look who it is!" he said, and his face lit up.

"Hello," said Jill. "I hope I'm not disturbing you . . ."

"Why no! I love some comp'ny while I tend me net. Sit!" he said, and gestured with his foot at an upturned bucket, still wet with the innards of gutted fish. Jill looked at it and remained standing.

"Was it you that lost your daughter to the sea?" Jill asked, even though she knew the answer.

The man's wide smile faded. He looked at Jill and his eyes were hollow. "Aye," he said. "'Twas."

Jill looked down. "I'm sorry," she said.

He nodded and sighed.

Jill looked back up, straight into the man's eyes, with a gaze sharper than a fish knife. "Are you trying to catch the mermaid?" she asked. Her mouth was set and her face was hard.

The man looked at her funny. "Lass," he said at last, "no man can cast such a net as can catch a mermaid."

Jill did not let him out of her gaze. He looked back down at his work on the net. "This poor rope and twine can no more catch a mermaid than you can catch the light o' the moon," he said. He began mending again. After a moment, Jill again said she was sorry for his loss, and started back toward the village. But after a dozen steps she glanced over her shoulder. The man was watching her darkly, keenly, from under his heavy brows. She hurried up the hill.

That night, Jill waited impatiently for Jack to fall asleep, and then, as soon as the mermaid's song began, she hurried down the steps and out the door of the tavern. As she slipped out into the night, she kept an eye on the little hut by the sea. Its door was tightly shut against the wind and the spray. As she made her way down to the rocks, though, following the sound of the mermaid's song, she thought she saw the door open just a crack. She stopped. She looked closer. Yes. The door to the bearded man's house was now standing ever so slightly ajar. Jill kept walking.

When she got to the little harbor, she walked on past it, farther out onto the rocks. The waves crashed around her feet as she climbed the slippery, craterous black crags out over the sea. At last she found a good footing.

"I didn't want him to see where I meet you," Jill whispered to the wind. "He's watching me right now."

As if in answer, the mermaid sang, *Never cry no more* again, and her song caught on the word *never*. The mermaid held it long and low and so sad, and then let it fall and gutter like waves

ADAM GIDWITZ

in a rocky shoal. The song ended. She did not pick it up again. Carefully, Jill walked back over the slick rocks, and then up the path and into the tavern. She closed the door behind her. She waited. Ten minutes later, she opened the door just a crack and peeked out. The bearded man's door was tightly shut.

Jack was sitting up when Jill awoke the next morning. "Hi!" he said. "I feel a lot better. I think I can help you with your work today."

Jill's hands instantly became clammy. She sat up and stared at him.

Then, as if deciding something, she got out of bed and came to his side. "Let me feel your head." The frog crawled out of the blankets and yawned sleepily. She put her hand on Jack's forehead. Compared to her clammy, sweating hands, Jack's forehead was smooth and dry and cool. "Take one more day," Jill said firmly. "One more day, and then you can come downstairs and help me."

"At least let me sit down there—" Jack began.

"No," said Jill, and her voice was sharp when she said it.

"I don't think sitting downstairs would be bad for Jack," the frog replied, surprised by her abruptness.

Jill thought for a moment. Then she said, "Not for Jack, no.

But I don't think the innkeeper would like him sitting in tavern, staring at the customers, do you? With a bandage on his head?" And without waiting for a response she got up, left the room, and closed the door behind her. Once in the corridor, she took a deep breath and went downstairs.

The lunch service in the tavern was always quiet, because the fishermen did not return with their boats until midafternoon. As soon as the last patron had left, Jill slipped out the tavern door and hurried down to the hut by the sea. The door was closed and no light came from within. The bearded man would, like the rest of the fishermen, be out on the sea for a couple of hours yet.

Jill went around to the back of the house. There, she tried the door of the shed. It wasn't locked. She slipped inside and closed the door behind her.

Within, she scanned the walls. Rusty instruments of death hung from every hook. She studied the hooked blade for opening a fish's belly, the sideways-bending knife for separating meat from bone, the harpoon points with their barbs that caught and tore the flesh. She found a coil of rope and set to work.

Now, my dear reader, you are probably feeling a little tense right now. If I've told this story well at all, in fact, you should be feeling a tightness in your shoulders, and a lightness in your head, and your breath should be coming a little quicker.

And when I describe Jill hiding in the hut with all the "instruments of death," as I think I called them—well, you are probably expecting something horrible and bloody to transpire.

Good. At least you're expecting it. That should help a little.

The bearded man came home exhausted and stinking of fish. He walked into his little house and peeled off his great oilskin coat and changed his heavy boots for some lighter shoes. Then, sighing from the day's work, he went out back and trudged heavily to his toolshed.

He pulled the door open and stepped inside—and found himself tumbling to the floor. His great frame crashed into the back wall, sending knives and knots and awls clattering down upon him. He looked back at the door. There was a rope tied tightly across the frame. He looked up.

Jill stood above him. Her face was furious and black. Her eyes were wide. Her nostrils flared. Her lips were pulled back around her teeth. Above her head hovered the largest, sharpest fish ax the man possessed.

"Leave the mermaid alone!" Jill bellowed.

And she brought the blade down as hard and as fast as she could. The man raised his arm to protect himself. The rusty blade hit his flesh with a *thwack* and buried itself in his bone. The man howled. Jill tried to pull the ax out, but it seemed to have become lodged there. Jill turned and grabbed the long, curving knife from the wall. She raised it and brought it down—but before it could enter the man's flesh, she was flung back by a kick to the chest. She tumbled over the rope and out into the daylight.

The man lay amid the fallen tools in the tiny shed, blood pouring from his arm onto the ground. He was staring at Jill.

"You leave her alone!" Jill snarled again, and then she ran.

Jill passed the tavern so quickly she did not see Jack looking out the window, watching her run up the road. Not that seeing him would have stopped her now. She kept going, up, up into the steep and misty hills. The wet grass was like a sponge beneath her feet. She could smell the peat smoke rising from the fires in the houses of the village. It was a sweet, musty smell. She passed a flock of sheep, lying on the green wet hillside. They bleated at her.

At the edge of the little valley behind the first hill, there stood a small sheepfold—just a wooden structure with three walls and a roof, where the sheep could gather if they wanted to get out of the rain. Jill made her way to that. She sat down in it.

ADAM GIDWITZ

She looked at herself. Her clothing was splattered with the man's blood.

She was sorry she hadn't killed him, but she thought that maybe, lying there, he might just bleed to death on his own. She thought of the beautiful mermaid—how perfect she was. And how she loved Jill. She loved her, Jill knew it. And to think that there had been six more of them, and that the bearded man had killed them all. It made her sick. And then, to think of his little daughter, who had died from grief because of him. Oh, what he had done to his little daughter.

Perhaps, she thought, she would return to his hut that night and be sure the job was done.

When the night was black, and Jill was certain that the people would have left the tavern and gone to their homes to sleep, Jill hurried back across the field of sheep, skirted around the edge of the silent fishing village, and made her way down to her little harbor. The mermaid was singing again. The song seemed to penetrate Jill's soul. It was intoxicating. It was unbearably beautiful.

> *Come, come, where heartache's never been.*
> *And where you're seen as you want to be seen.*
> *Come, come, the place of shadow and green,*

Where you'll never cry no more, dear lass,

Where you'll never cry no more.

Jill's vision became blurred. She couldn't see the houses of the village, nor the sky above it. All she could see was the black, heaving ocean and the craterous, craggy rocks that rose up around it, like teeth around a great mouth. The mermaid was singing more sweetly and sadly than she ever had before. Jill came to the water's edge. She looked out at the mermaid's rock, surrounded by the spuming, frothing ocean, but the mermaid was not there.

"Here," she heard. Jill looked down. There, directly below Jill, just beneath the surface of the sea, the mermaid floated. Jill bent over and, staring down at the mermaid, it felt like she was staring into a mirror of obsidian, and the mermaid was her beautiful, perfected reflection. *If only the mermaid really were Jill's reflection*, she thought. If only. She wanted it so badly it made her heart ache.

The mermaid's eyes were wider and blacker and greener than Jill had remembered, and her hair that looked like the shining of the moon on the water at night blew every which way under the waves. And she was smiling at Jill.

"Beautiful girl," she said from under the water. "Beautiful, brave girl. You have done something to defend me, and to avenge my sisters. I can feel it."

Jill sat down on the edge of the rocks. She folded her feet behind her and dangled her fingers in the cold, wild water. "I tried," Jill said. "I tried to."

The mermaid beamed at her. "You beautiful, brave girl. Here," she said, "let me kiss you." And then she was rising up out of the water, her white body shining in the moonlight, her green and black scales shimmering darkly below. She raised her face to Jill's face and brought her foamy lips to Jill's left cheek. Jill felt them brush against her skin, and it was the softest, sweetest feeling she had ever felt. She closed her eyes. Above her, a great black wave rose into the night.

The great wave rose, and then paused.

And then it came crashing down upon the mermaid and little girl. It slammed Jill's body into the sharp rocks. It dragged her, with an irresistible pull, down, down, down. Jill tried kicking, fighting it, but she just sank deeper beneath the waves. She opened her mouth to scream, and water rushed into her lungs. She opened her eyes and they burned from the salt. But she could see. She could see the beautiful mermaid, holding on to her wrists, her face contorted, demented. And behind the mermaid, Jill could see six other mermaids, rushing toward her, their faces twisted, warped. And they sang as their hands grabbed at Jill's arms, Jill's legs, Jill's hair. They sang:

> Come, come, where heartache's never been.
> And where you're seen as you want to be seen.
> Come, come, the place of shadow and green,
> Where you'll never cry no more, dear lass,
> Where you'll never cry no more.

And finally, Jill saw the body of a little girl, tangled among the seaweed at the rocky bottom of the harbor. The body was pale, and it floated lifelessly, its eyes staring up unseeing toward the surface.

It was a lie. The mermaid had lied.

The last breath left Jill, the last fight died in her arms and legs and lungs. She went limp. The sea grew dark.

And then, falling through the darkling sea, there was a net. It fell and fell, sliding over the mermaids as if they were not there, as if they were no more than beams of the moon. But it fell around Jill and cradled her, and it pulled her up, up, away from the mermaids' grasping hands, up to the surface of the water, up above the obsidian waves and into the moonlight and the freezing, bracing air.

ADAM GIDWITZ

Jill was placed gently on the rocks and the net was opened. She coughed and coughed, seawater pouring out of her mouth. She held herself up with her hands and retched until every last drop of brine was purged. Then, drained, Jill sat back.

A pair of arms draped themselves over her. Small, thin arms. Jill opened her eyes. She could see only a white bandage. Then she felt amphibian skin on her neck.

She looked up, over the bandage that was nestled under her chin, and saw that the big-bellied man with the red beard was staring at her, shaking his head. He looked like he was crying. "I got ya this time," he whispered, as if to himself. "This time, I got ya."

The bandage pulled back. It was Jack, holding the frog in his hands. Little Jack was smiling tearfully. The red-bearded man approached and picked Jill up, cradling her, with his one good arm, away from the bandaged one, and carried her back toward the tavern. "I told ya," he said to her as he walked, Jack following just a pace behind. "No man can cast such a net as can catch a mermaid. But a mermaid can surely cast such a net as can catch a little girl."

The man with the red beard was all better now. His arm had been in a sling for a few weeks, and each night he removed his bandages and rubbed it with a local whisky. He said that was better than any doctor could do.

His heart was better, too. But he didn't need any whisky for that. The innkeeper told Jill that, for the first time since his daughter had died, the man with the red beard was his old self again. "I got her," you could hear him say to himself. "This time, I got her."

The man treated Jack like a son. Jack, who had watched Jill go down to the little hut, who had seen the man come home from the fishing boats, who had wondered at Jill sprinting away past the inn. Jack had tried running out of the inn after her, but he hadn't seen where she had gone. All that had been left to do was go down to the little hut. He had found the bearded man, unconscious in the shed, still bleeding. "He saved m' life," the bearded man said after they'd told Jill the story. "And yours, too."

The days were fine, there in the little village by the sea, and the people had grown to love Jack and Jill. But the children had to move on, for they were no closer to the Seeing Glass.

And besides, the mermaid still sang at night, tormenting Jill with her beautiful song.

So the children asked the red-bearded man if he knew where they could find goblins.

The man's face grew dark. "Why would you want to see the goblins? It's an evil race, the goblins are."

"We're looking for a mirror," said Jill. "The Seeing Glass. It's in the deepest part of the earth."

The man smoothed his red beard with his meaty hand. He shook his head. "If it's the belly of the earth you want—ay, the goblins could show you there. But they're more likely to trap you, and kill you, and sell you for parts."

Jack started, but Jill just set her jaw and said, "Where are they?"

The man heaved himself to his feet and walked with the children out of the tavern. Through the morning mist, he pointed out into the hills. "The Goblin Market is that way."

The children embraced the big man with the red beard, and then set out into the steep green hills behind the village. They walked away from the small seaside village, away from the sea, away from the tall green hill, and if their sense of direction deceived them not, far, far away from home.

CHAPTER SIX

The Gray Valley

O nce upon a time, a boy named Jack, a girl named Jill, and a frog named Frog stumbled through high mountains and rocky valleys in a land very far away from the kingdom of Märchen. They were tired; they were hungry; they were thirsty; and they were sick to death of walking.

The sky was as gray as the loose stones that lay on the sides of the mountains, which was as gray as the sodden sod in the shallow valleys. The wind blew cold and wet, and would have been gray, too, if wind had a color.

At last, Jack, Jill, and the frog collapsed on their backs on a wide, smooth stone, and wondered if they were dead yet.

"So hungry," Jill moaned.

"So thirsty," Jack groaned.

"So worried," said the frog. "I hope we don't starve to death."

"Yes," said Jill, "not starving to death would be nice."

"So would not thirsting to death," said Jack.

"Thirsting isn't even a word," said Jill.

"It isn't?"

"No."

"Then what's the word?"

"I don't know. Dying of thirst."

"You can starve to death. Why can't you thirst to death?"

"I don't know. You just can't."

"Oh."

This is, of course, the kind of inane conversation that occurs when people are slowly losing their minds.

Through it, the frog was staring up at the sky, as he used to do when he lived in his well. For not the first time in that frog's long life, he was wishing he were back in it, salamanders and all. He could hear them now: "What is smelly?" "When is smelly?" "Why is smelly?" "Who is smelly?" "Am I smelly?" "Who's smellier, me or Fred? Is it me? It's me, right? Me?" He sort of missed them.

"Frog, I have a question," said Jack, who was now lying on his back, staring at the sky.

"Shoot."

"How do you talk?"

Jill looked over at Jack, and then at the frog. "Yeah," she said.

The frog sighed. He purposely did *not* look at Jill. "It's kind of a long story."

"Okay," said Jack.

"Okay," said Jill.

"Okay what?" said the frog.

"Okay, tell us the story," Jack answered.

The frog thought about it for a minute. He continued to purposely *not* look at Jill. And then, at last, he said, "All right . . ."

So the frog told them the story of how he came to talk. He started with the very smelly well, moved on to the very annoying salamanders, then described the princess with her ball, and so on, all the way through him trailing his froggy blood after him, all the way back to his well.

When he'd finished, Jack said. "That's a good story."

"Thank you," said the frog.

"My favorite part was when your leg got eaten by the weasel," Jack added.

The frog did not thank him again.

But Jill was silent. She stared into the great gray sky. After a long time, she said, "I think that was my mother."

The frog watched her. Jill said nothing more. But the frog could tell she was thinking. Thinking hard.

The frog glanced up. Three black specks had appeared through the heavy cloud. He watched them as the specks grew into dots, and the dots into blots, and the blots into splotches, and the splotches into birds, and the birds, at last, into ravens.

The frog catapulted himself out of Jack's pocket and dove for a dark crevice beneath a stone. Jack and Jill gazed at him like he was crazy. Then they heard the wings.

They looked up in time to see three black shapes fluttering down and landing on the stone beside them. The children stared. Three large and stately ravens shook their plumage and stood, dark and imperious, before them.

A vague sense of dread took hold of the children.

"What do you think they want?" Jack whispered.

"I know what they want," Jill whispered back. "They're scavengers. They're here to eat us after we die."

"What?" cried one of the ravens.

Jill toppled over backward.

Jack ducked as if something were about to strike him in the head.

"What did she just say we were going to do?" demanded another raven.

Jack's eyes were spread wide. Jill's head tilted wonderingly off to one side.

"They said we were going to eat their corpses," the third raven replied.

"That is the most repulsive thing I have heard in many, many years," declared the first.

"Did that raven just *talk*?" Jill hissed at Jack.

"I think they all did," he whispered back.

"Why are you whispering?" whispered the second raven. "We can hear, too, you know."

Jack and Jill silently wondered if they were hallucinating.

"Really, I'm not sure why you're so surprised," said the third raven. "You travel with a talking frog."

"Speaking of whom . . ." said the second. The frog was still trying to fit in the crevice between the rock and the ground. Really, he was not slim enough and just didn't seem to want to admit it.

"What is he doing?" asked the third.

"I imagine he's afraid of us," said the first. "We do eat frogs."

The frog's three legs kicked and scrabbled with renewed energy at the dirt beneath the stone. Jack reached out and scooped him up and put him in his pocket.

"You can't eat him," he said, glaring at the ravens.

"Don't even think about it!" added Jill fiercely. And then, a little less fiercely, she said, "And how did you know he can talk?"

"We know things," said the first raven.

"Yes," said the second, "It's sort of what we *do*."

Jill, crinkling up her nose, asked, "Like what kinds of things?"

"We know that you are Jack and Jill," said the third raven.

"And that you are hungry and thirsty and lost," said the second.

"And that you seek the Seeing Glass," finished the first.

The frog poked a single eye out of Jack's pocket. "Do they know where it is?" he hissed.

"Do you know where it is?" Jack relayed to the ravens.

"Yeah, we heard him," said the second raven.

"We know where it is—" began the first.

"Where?"

"But we're not telling," concluded the third.

"What?!" Jack shouted. "Why not?"

"Because the Seeing Glass," said the second raven, "is not really what you seek."

No one spoke for a moment. The wind howled over the slick rocks and gray hills.

And then Jill said, "Yes it is. If we don't find it, we *die*."

The wind howled for another moment, and then the second raven said, "Right. I suppose that's true."

"But, dear children, you are con-fused," said the third raven.

"Absolutely," said the second.

"Totally," said the first.

Jill said, "If you'd just met three talking ravens, wouldn't you be?"

"Not really," said the third talking raven.

But the first raven said, "Not *confused*. You are *con-fused*."

Jack furrowed his brow. "What's the difference?"

"We're glad you asked," replied the second raven.

And the third added, "Though we knew you would."

"When you're confused," said the second raven, "you're mixed up, right?"

"Right," said Jack.

"Well, *con-fuse* means fused together, mixed with something—or someone—else." The second raven paused significantly.

After a moment, Jill said, "I still have no idea what you're talking about."

The first raven took over: "You, dear children, are con-fused. What you want, what you think, what you believe, all get mixed up with what other people want for you, or think you should want, or believe about you. Do you see?"

Both Jack and Jill nodded their heads and said, "No."

The third raven took over. "Jill, you are con-fused with your mother. You think she is perfect, and that everything she does is good, and that you should be just like her and do just what she wants you to do. Right?"

Jill's mouth grew tight and small. She shrugged.

"Did you see the silk?"

Shrug.

"Did you really think you'd look beautiful in it? Before your mother said you would?"

Shrug.

The third raven turned to Jack. "Jack, why did you trade your cow for a bean?"

Jack looked up at the raven heavily. He, too, shrugged.

"Did you think it was a good deal before Marie said it was?"

Shrug.

"When is the last time you disagreed with something the boys from the village said or did?"

Shrug.

"Children!" the third raven exclaimed, exasperated now, "You are con-fused. Totally, utterly con-fused. As long as you are, you will never find what you seek. Even though it's right here."

Jack scrunched up his face and looked all around him.

Jill looked down at herself and then back up the ravens.

"When you do what you want, not what you wish . . ." said the first raven.

"When you no longer seek your reflection in others' eyes . . ." said the second.

"When you see yourselves face to face . . ." said the third.

"Then," the ravens intoned in unison, "you will have found what you truly seek."

Jack and Jill glanced at each other.

Jill said, "Do you know what they're talking about?"

"No idea," Jack replied.

They turned to ask for further explanation, but the three black forms were already whirling high into the air. The two children, and the frog, watched as the ravens shrank and shrank against the immense gray sky, until, finally, three black specks disappeared into the clouds.

"That was weird," said Jill.

"Yeah," said Jack.

After a moment, the frog asked, "What should we do now?"

Jill said, "I don't know, but I am thirsting to death."

Jack agreed. "And I'm about to die of starve."

CHAPTER SEVEN

Goblin
Market

Once upon a time, a boy and a girl and a frog stood at the peak of a mountain, looking out over a great valley. Two broad roads wound from the distance into the bowl of the valley, forming a crossroads right at its center. All around the crossroads, and spreading out over what must have been a hundred acres, was something that hit the two children like a punch to all their senses at once. If you can imagine what a punch to your senses might feel like.

Once they got over the shock of it, they recognized it for what it was. It was a market. The most fantastic market that has ever been. Fragrances rose to their nostrils and beckoned them. Sweet music floated on the air and called to them. Bright flags and fabrics flapped gently in the suddenly warm wind.

Jack and Jill threw themselves down the scree slope, slipping and laughing and sliding on their bottoms, until they reached the foot of the mountain. They began to cross the flat floor of the valley. Soon they came to a stone buried in the earth. Inscribed upon the stone were words. They read:

Come in, come in, we'll make you a buyer.

Jack and Jill, not knowing what to make of it, walked on. After a few yards they came to another stone. This one said:

We have everything anyone's ever desired.

They looked up at the market. It seemed bigger than it had just a moment ago. It smelled better, too.

Ten feet on, they came to another stone. It read:

You'll feel like you're floating higher and higher.

The market looked even bigger now. They walked on and came to another stone.

When you finally get what you've always desired,

ADAM GIDWITZ

They glanced up again, and the market had burgeoned out to the horizon, its poles and flags piercing the sky. Soon, they came to yet another stone:

Your life seems to sink into deepening mire—

Jack and Jill were pretty sure they knew what "mire" was going to rhyme with. Sure enough, the next stone said,

Why do you let it? Take what you desire!

They weren't far from the edge of the market now. It thrummed before them like the great ocean itself, beckoning them, calling them. They plunged in.

Jack and Jill found themselves in the midst of the most magnificent market you can possibly imagine.

Go ahead, try to imagine the most magnificent market you possibly can.

Have you?

All right. Not good enough. Not even close.

First of all, was the market you were imagining filled with *goblins*?

Oh, it was?

Okay.

But did it have stalls selling gemstones and gold ingots the size of your head?

Did it have stacks of coins, bronze and silver and gold, crazily stretching far above the merchant men?

Were there carpets that levitated, tapestries that danced, and silks that appeared and disappeared depending on the angle of the light?

Was there food of every shape and size and smell and taste and color, from buttery star-shaped cakes to spits of meat that dripped golden oil?

Was there a mechanical menagerie, where tigers and peacocks and crocodiles, all made from gears and pistons but covered in real fur or feathers or skin, moved around and growled and squawked and grunted?

Did the market you imagined have all that?

It did?

Oh.

Fine.

Well, what do you need me for? Go ahead and imagine the rest of the chapter yourself.

ADAM GIDWITZ

Okay, I'm done pouting.

So Jack and Jill walked through this magnificent market, marveling at the gemstones and the gold, the dancing tapestries, the succulent food, the mechanical beasts.

But mostly, they marveled at the goblins.

The goblins, you see, were all grown men, and yet none was taller than either Jack or Jill. They had deep black eyes with no whites at all. And lank black hair. But their skin was the strangest thing about them. It was a pale green—not so green that you would confuse it with key lime pie; nor so pale that you'd think they were just seasick. About halfway in between key lime pie and seasick. That was the color of the goblins' skin.

Now if you've ever read books with goblins, or seen movies with goblins, or even played video games with goblins, you will want to tell me that I am wrong, and that goblins, in fact, do not look at all as I have described them. You will want to tell me that goblins have hunched backs, red eyes, pointy ears and chins, sharp teeth, and skin that is very very very green.

You must know that this image you have of goblins is a terrible lie. It was first circulated by a powerful and ubiquitous crayon company who shall here remain nameless, when they discovered that, try as they might, they could not make a shade of green that matched the tone of a goblin's skin. They made it too light, and the goblins looked seasick; they made it too dark, and they looked like slices of key lime pie. "Goblin green?" they said. "Impossible!" So they started telling kids that, really, that bright green that already came in the box was just the right color, and, as an added bonus, the bright red was the perfect color for the eyes. And you know what? All the kids believed them. I bet you did, too.

Well, now you know better. Pale green skin. And, as I said, deep black eyes, with no whites at all, and lank black hair that they treat in all different kinds of ways—side part, ponytail, comb-over to hide balding, and so on. Their faces were all different, but every one looked like a man of about fifty or fifty-five—some fat, some thin, but all tired, overworked.

And hungry. For something.

Jack and Jill moved deeper and deeper into the Goblin Market. It seemed to go on forever. The children walked as if in a daze, their eyes passing limply over wonders too wonderful even to describe. As they walked, the eyes of the goblins followed them.

ADAM GIDWITZ

From behind signs, from under awnings, from within brightly colored pavilions, the goblins watched the two human children, their dark eyes following them, step by innocent step.

Suddenly, Jack heard a clanging sound. It rose from a ramp that seemed to lead down into the earth. At the very same moment, Jill heard a chanting, pulsing cry:

Come buy our orchard fruits,
Come buy! Come buy!

The calls came from a section of the market filled with fruits stalls. Tables were stacked high with pyramids of big black grapes, domes of blood oranges, tangles of ruby cherries. Behind or beside each table, goblins called out their song:

Apples and quinces! Melons and raspberries!
All ripe together
In summer weather!

Jill's mouth began to water. "Jack!" she cried. "We have to go to the fruit market!"

But Jack was already wandering in the direction of the ramp that led down into the earth.

Jill didn't notice. She started toward the fruit sellers. They called out, their goblin voices straining:

Grapes fresh from the vine,
Pomegranates full and fine!

Jill entered the fruit stalls. The goblin men watched her from beneath heavy brows. Their tables were loaded with sweet smelling fruit. Jill passed her hand over glossy apples and delicately fingered puckered raspberries. The goblin men smiled at her from their dark, hungry eyes. Their calls became louder, more insistent:

Figs to fill your mouth,
Citrons from the South,
Sweet to tongue and sound to eye!
Come buy!
Come buy!

The goblin men watched Jill's hand trail across their fruits. They whispered to one another, pointed, smiled.

Suddenly, a goblin called out: "Hello, my pretty!"

Then another said, "Good day, my lovely!"

"Hello there, beauty."

"Darling girl, have a peach! Eat my peaches!"

"Or my pears, sweet one!"

"Red cherries for a beautiful girl!"

Young Jill looked up at the strange, leering men. Her heart beat an uncertain pattern in her chest.

"My lovely!"

"Pretty one!"

"Come eat my fruits!"

"Eat mine!"

"Eat mine!"

And then one goblin slid out from behind his stall, an apple in his hand. Jill stopped. He came toward her, closer and closer, until his body was brushing against hers, and his face was inches from her own. She could smell him. She felt strange.

"A lovely apple for a lovely girl?" he asked. And he raised its red flesh to her nose. Jill closed her eyes and drew the scent in. It was rich and tempting.

"Sweet, isn't it?" he asked.

Her eyes still shut, Jill nodded.

The goblin said, "Take a bite."

Jill opened her eyes. She saw the old goblin face, his skin so close to hers, his dark eyes drinking her in. And in those eyes, she saw her own reflection. She suddenly thought of other reflections she had seen—in her mother's mirror, in the sea.

Something felt wrong.

"No," she said, and she pushed the apple away.

But more goblins had come out from behind their stalls. They were moving closer and closer, watching the fruit seller and Jill. They began crowding in on her, with their heat and their smell. Soon they were pressing in upon her, jostling her, pushing her, holding her.

"Pretty girl! Eat my fruit!"

"No, mine!"

"Mine, my beauty! Mine!"

She felt confused. They were saying nice things, and yet . . .

"My lovely one!"

"My darling!"

"Eat! Eat!"

They licked their dry lips with muscular tongues and pushed in closer to Jill, and closer.

"Stop!" she cried suddenly. "Get away!" The goblins' sweat clouded Jill's nostrils. She could feel their thick, rough hands on her hair. "Get away from me!"

But they would not. They pressed closer and closer and closer.

"Jack!" Jill cried. "JACK!"

Jack stood in front of one of the dark entrances that led underground. He heard his name. He turned. A mountain of goblins seethed in the center of what appeared to be a fruit market.

"JACK!"

He squinted his eyes and took a step toward it.

"JACK!"

He saw one of Jill's thin hands appear above the goblins' heads.

He began to run.

Inside the scrum of goblins, Jill pushed and kicked and shouted.

"Pretty girl!" they cried.

"Beautiful one!"

"Come with us!"

"Be with us!"

"NO!" she shouted. "GET AWAY!" She turned her head this way and that as the goblins tried to push peaches and pears and plums past her lips. "JACK!" she screamed.

And just as she did, a muscular goblin with a vicious face shoved an apple into her mouth. She tried to tear her face away, but as she moved, her teeth pierced the apple's flesh.

And Jill collapsed.

Jack pushed at the backs of the thronging goblins frantically, trying to shove his way to his cousin. But the goblins were surprisingly strong. An arm thrust Jack backward. He pushed into the scrum of goblins again. "Jill!" he shouted. "JILL!"

And then he saw Jill, lifted up by a dozen goblin arms, being borne aloft and carried away. She looked dead.

"JILL!" he cried. He tried to follow her. But he could not penetrate the iron cord of goblin arms. Jack watched, helplessly, as Jill was swept into one of the dark openings in the earth, and out of sight.

"We've got to follow her!" the frog screamed. "We've got to save her!"

The dust of the ground mingled with the acrid-sweet smells of the fruit market.

"I know," said Jack. He squinted against the bright sun. "I know."

Jack stood on a ramp that descended into the ground. He looked out over the rest of the Goblin Market—an underground market.

Stalls and huts of clanging metal stretched into the dark distance under a towering ceiling of black stone. The frog shoved his fingers in his ears against the incessant *clang clang clang* of the smithy stalls. The underground market was even more teeming with life and strangeness than its counterpart aboveground. A thousand stalls stretched out into the distance, and among them wove goblins with baskets and bags of goods. Beyond the market, far, far in the distance, were taller buildings.

There was no sign of Jill, or of the band of goblins that had carried her away. They had disappeared like the smoke of a forge into a low-hanging fog.

But Jack had to start somewhere. He descended into the darkness, asking goblins as he went, "Have you seen a girl? A human girl? Being carried by goblins? Have you seen her? Has anyone seen her?"

No one had.

Jack wandered on and on and on, past stalls with metal trinkets, axes of glowing iron, tiny daggers no bigger than Jack's pinkie. And swords. Wonderful, deadly, beautiful swords.

Jack saw a two-handed broadsword that hung in front of one of the shops. It had a long thick blade and a rounded tip. He wondered how much it cost. Not that he had any money. But still, he was curious. He examined its cross-guard, and found, dangling from it, a thread of leather with a small piece of parchment at the end. *One Hand*, the parchment read.

"Jack," said the frog, "come on. We need to find Jill."

Jack let go of the cryptic message and backed away from the stall.

Just a few steps farther along, he saw another sword, with gold filigree all the way up the blade, and he thought, *No, that's the one for me.* This sword had no parchment attached to it. So Jack said to the crook-backed goblin who stood nearby, conversing with another weapon-smith, "How much for this sword?"

"One hand," said the goblin, as if this was obvious, and turned back to his conversation. Jack considered asking for an explanation. But he could not think of any possible explanation of the price "one hand" that would make him able to afford it.

"Jack!" cried the frog. "Come on!"

"Right," said Jack. "Sorry. I was just—" But he stopped there, for hanging from a rack of daggers was a tiny dirk—a thin, steeply graded blade on a guardless handle. It was gorgeous.

A wooden, hand-painted plaque hung above the rack of daggers. It read, ALL DAGGERS, ONE HAND. Jack stood before the sign.

The frog was about to shout at Jack again, but a goblin with a sallow, thin face and a little paunch of a belly asked Jack if he liked what he saw.

"I do," said Jack. "But I don't understand. What does this mean, 'One Hand'?"

"What do you think?" said the goblin, his long goblin fingers tapping his sagging paunch.

"I don't know," Jack replied.

"Sure you do," the goblin said. Jack, alarmed and confused, turned and moved on.

The frog was pleading now: "Jack, we have to find Jill."

Jack shook himself as if he'd been asleep. What was wrong with him? He felt as if a fog were before his eyes. Jill had been stolen! *Come on!* he thought. *Wake up! Go find her!*

And then he saw a small clearing among the weapon-smiths. In the center of the clearing, on a stone altar, was a sword lying on a blanket of crushed velvet. Its blade was about the length of Jack's arm. Its handle was iron wrapped in leather. Its cross-guard was simplicity itself, and its pommel was just an iron ball. It was neither long nor short, bright nor dull, new nor old.

And yet there was something about the sword that was different from the others that Jack had seen. There seemed to be nothing special about it, Jack thought, except that it looked exactly as he had always believed a sword should look. In fact, he suspected that he recognized it from somewhere.

Jack walked up to it. He circled the table. He reached for it. It seemed to leap into his hand, like metal filings to a magnet. Jack admired it. Then he recognized it.

It looked just like the sword he wielded in his dreams.

"It likes you," said a goblin who was suddenly standing by his shoulder. "That is a good sign."

Jack held it, and it felt like an extension of his arm. "It's perfect," Jack said.

"Jack!" hissed the frog.

"That's right," said the goblin. "It is the sword you've always dreamed of. Go ahead," he smiled. "Give it a try."

Jack nodded and stepped back from the table. He whipped the sword through the air. The wind seemed to sing with its passing. All the goblins at all the stalls nearby stopped what they were doing and turned to look at Jack. He swung it again. The goblins' black eyes silently followed the motion of the sword.

The frog pushed his head out of Jack's pocket. "Jack, can you hear me?"

Jack did not reply.

"What do you want to be, my boy?" the goblin asked.

And without hesitation, without even realizing he was saying it, Jack said, "I want to be respected."

"With that sword, you will be feared by all," the goblin assured him.

Jack thrust the sword again. "I want to be admired," Jack said, more forcefully this time.

ADAM GIDWITZ

"You will be!" said the goblin. "You will be!"

"Jack?" cried the frog.

Jack spun with the sword and cut the air. He was shouting. *"I want everyone to like me!"*

"Oh, they will! They will!" cried the goblin. "Everyone will like you!" And then he added, "And it will only cost your hand."

Jack saw himself stabbing a boy who looked quite a lot like Marie—when the sword point dipped. He let it come to rest on the ground. Slowly, he turned to the goblin. "What does that mean?" he asked. "I don't understand."

"Not a single gold piece. Not a single copper. Nothing but your hand." Then the goblin added, "Your left one, of course! Not your sword hand!" And he smiled, like he was doing Jack a favor.

Okay, I've got a question for you.

If the goblin is lying, and the sword is just a normal sword, trading your *hand* for it is probably a bad deal. Right?

But I can tell you right now—and I know this from my extensive research on the subject—that the goblin is *not* lying.

Anyone who gives up his hand for a goblin sword will gain all the power of the sword. This sword will give Jack what he has always most desired. Quite truly.

And it will only cost his left hand.

Think of what you most desire. Really think of it.

Okay.

Would you give your hand for it?

Jack stood and stared at the goblin man. It had felt like a game, playing with the sword, until now.

Until he knew that he could have it.

And that it had a price.

"Uh, Jack . . ." said the frog. "Jack . . . is this a joke?"

The goblin man said, "You will be admired by everyone . . . *everyone* . . ." Then he said, "You could give your right hand, if it's easier to part with."

"Everyone would like me . . . *everyone* . . ." Jack murmured.

"Jack, can you hear me?" the frog pleaded. "Jack, this is crazy! It's just a sword . . . Let's find Jill and get out of here . . ."

But Jack did not hear him. He was saying, "They will like me. They will love me. They will fear me . . ." He knew it was true. He could feel the sword's power humming up his arm.

"Jack! JACK!" The frog shouted.

Jack gripped the sword firmly in his right hand.

He looked levelly at the goblin.

Jack nodded.

"Get the apothecary!" the goblin shouted. In a moment an apothecary appeared, a short squat goblin with a black carrying case. He came and took some bottles and bandages from his bag.

The frog was screaming, "STOP IT, JACK, STOP IT!"

Jack paid no attention. "Put your left hand on the velvet," said the goblin sword-smith. Jack placed his left hand on the velvet.

"With your right hand, raise the sword into the air," said the goblin. With his right hand, Jack raised the sword into the air.

"When you're ready, you may cut off your left hand," said the goblin.

Jack's heart caught.

"*Don't do it*," the frog whispered frantically. "*Jack, you will be sorry. So, so sorry.*"

Jack thought of Marie, laughing at him. He thought of his father. *It'll prove that you're a man.* He held his breath.

The blade began to sing.

CHAPTER EIGHT

Death or the Lady

O nce upon a time, a girl—limp and unconscious—
was carried through the underground darkness of the Goblin
Kingdom. She was brought to a massive black palace. It had tall,
spindly towers that seemed to have been shaped by the slow drip-
drip-drip of underground water. Wings and annexes extended
from its center like great black spiders' legs. Banners of many
colors flew from the ramparts and towers—but in the darkness of
the earth, each looked merely like the fluttering shadows of colors.
In each of the thousand windows, an orange flame flickered.

But Jill did not see the towering black castle. She was, as I
said, unconscious.

She did not feel herself passed from the strong hands of

the fruit merchants into the even stronger hands of the goblin guards. She did not know that she was being carried through dark hallways deep in the belly of the castle that stood deep in the belly of the earth. She did not see the goblin with the careworn face and the deep, old eyes examining her. She did not feel the heat of his skin so near he could have kissed her, nor did she smell the stale breath of his mouth. She did not hear him call to a dour goblin who waited in a corner; she did not hear the latches of an ornate case snap open; she did not see the long, strange instrument withdrawn from the case; she did not see its sharp end slowly, so slowly, approach her closed eyelids.

If she had, she doubtless would have screamed.

She did not perceive—either by feeling or by sight—the gentle application of makeup to her face with the long, strange instrument. Not of blue to her eyelids nor blush to her cheeks nor red to her lips. She did not know that her hair was being brushed by gentle goblin hands. She did not feel the coolness of the dank air on her body as she was undressed and redressed in the finest silks. She did not feel herself lifted again.

The first thing that Jill did feel was a pinching tightness on her wrists and ankles. Her eyes were still closed, and she felt woozy. The second thing she felt was that she could not open her mouth. Her eyes flew open.

She was sitting on a high throne in the center of an enormous hall. The ceiling towered overhead. The black stone walls were decked with enormous tapestries thirty feet high. Before her, twenty goblins, clad in plate metal and carrying spears, stood with their backs toward her, and beyond them, in single file, stood a line of goblin men so long it wound straight out of the enormous hall.

Jill tried to open her mouth again and discovered that a broad bolt of fine silk had pinned her lips shut. She tried to lift her hands to remove the gag and found that they were tied with the same fine silk to the arms of the throne. She tried to stand up and found that her ankles were tied to the throne, too.

"She is awake!" announced a goblin with a rich voice, a careworn face, and deep, old eyes.

The long line of goblins began to move. Jill watched in mute fear as the first came before her throne. He wore a bright green velvet suit which clashed hideously with his pale green skin. He swept a giant green hat with an enormous yellow feather from his head. He smiled up at Jill and said, "Your Majesty, you are beautiful."

Jill felt very confused. *Your Majesty?*

The goblin smiled more broadly. "You are bright like the moon and beautiful like a flower. I see you, and my heart aches."

Despite herself, and despite everything else—the bonds, the gag, the apparent kidnapping—Jill blushed.

The next goblin, festooned with silver fabric, announced, "My Queen, you shine like a diamond." He gazed up into her face. Under his breath, he said, "I have never seen anyone so beautiful."

Jill's cheeks grew hot, and she looked away.

The third goblin told Jill he was stunned by her perfect features. Jill was shocked to discover that, beneath the silken gag, she was smiling.

The fourth goblin said that, now that he had seen her, he would dream of her at night. Again, Jill blushed hotly. The fifth goblin admired every single feature of her face. "Your nose is like a small hill, bright and clean. Your cheeks are like pink pillows. Your hair looks like grass. Brown grass. Your head is shaped like a . . ." And so on. Jill giggled to think of someone taking so much interest in the shape of her head.

But by the ninth goblin, Jill was bored.

By the fifteenth goblin, she was testing her silken bonds again.

And by the twenty-eighth goblin, Jill did not care *what* they thought of her.

Which she found very surprising.

ADAM GIDWITZ

Because, at long last, Jill was being admired—worshipped—for her beauty.

Just as she had always wanted.

And, it turned out, she did not like it at all.

The fortieth goblin did not praise her beauty. Instead, he threw himself on the ground and cried, "Queen, I am devoted to you! You are as rare as ivory, as fresh as the spring. I will risk my very life to be your husband. Will you have me?"

Jill stared. She didn't know what to say. Then she remembered that she couldn't say anything because she was gagged.

But she didn't need to. For there was a sudden movement. Two guards had stepped forward from the line of twenty that stood before the throne. They approached the goblin-suitor and slammed the butts of their spears into the stone floor. They barked: "Will you risk your life to treasure and protect this lady?"

"I will! I will!" cried the goblin.

"Bring forth the casket!" the goblin guards yelled. Four other guards came forward with a great iron casket, suspended between two long poles. "In this casket," barked the guards, every syllable perfectly in time, "are two slips of parchment. One says 'Death!' The other says 'The Lady!' If you choose 'Death!' you will be killed right here on the spot! If you choose 'The Lady!'

you will become her husband for all the rest of your days, and you and she will spend countless hours together alone, engaging in whatever pursuits give her pleasure. Do you understand?"

"God, yes!" the goblin screamed. "Let me choose!"

Jill, on the other hand, did *not* understand. She fought her silken bonds.

"Submit to blindfolding!" the guards barked, and the goblin was blindfolded. The two soldiers moved behind the blindfolded goblin-suitor and pointed their spears at his back.

The casket was brought directly before the suitor.

Can they make me marry him? Jill thought frantically. *They can't, right?*

The casket was opened. The goblin-suitor reached in.

He withdrew a small piece of parchment.

He held it before his blindfolded face, his expression contorted with grotesque excitement. Jill stared at him and felt sick.

The goblin tore off his blindfold and examined the paper.

"No!" he screamed, and the two goblin guards standing behind him rammed their spears straight through his body with a horrible crunching, slicing sound. The spear points came out, red and covered in viscera, on the other side. The goblin collapsed—quite dead—on the floor.

I'm sorry. I forgot to warn you that was coming. I was too caught up in telling the story. Anyway, it's all over now.

Jill, seeing the dead goblin, felt a mix of horror and relief that she found very confusing.

Four goblins ran out from who-knew-where and picked up the corpse and scrubbed the floor clean. All remnants of the hapless suitor were removed, and the line continued as it had before.

A few more admirers came and went. And then, another goblin threw himself on the ground and proclaimed his undying love for Jill.

Jill started in alarm and tried frantically to rip herself from the throne, to save either herself from marriage or the goblin from death.

But the two goblin soldiers came forward and questioned him, and then the four goblins came out with the casket.

Again the goblin drew a piece of parchment from the great chest.

Again, he held it before his blindfolded face as he quivered with excitement.

And again, he removed his blindfold, examined the paper, screamed in agony, and the two spears were rammed through his back. Blood spurted out of his chest as if from a fountain, spraying the casket and the two guards and then, once he had collapsed, dribbling slowly out of his body and running among the cobblestones.

Sorry, sorry! Totally forgot! Last time! Promise!

The four goblins on cleanup duty came forth and scrubbed the floor with red rags, and a minute later, the line was moving again.

Jill felt sick to her stomach.

Goblin after goblin told Jill of her celestial, supernatural, otherworldly beauty. They stared into her face and simpered lovingly at her.

She found it revolting.

And every third or fourth goblin declared his undying love for her, was presented with the casket, and was summarily killed.

After the fifteenth goblin had been stabbed through his

back, Jill began to have serious doubts about the fairness of the test. It seemed to her that if there were two slips of parchment in the casket, one saying "Death!" and the other "The Lady!", she would be married to half the goblins in the room by now.

Three goblins in a row all declared their undying love for Jill, and all of them died on the points of spears. The last one convulsed on the floor, screaming in pain, as blood bubbled up out of his body like a hot spring and flowed all over the floor in crimson waves, eventually lapping up against the throne's legs like water against rocks on a beach.

Jeez! My bad! Sorry!

Jill stared. *How is it possible,* she wondered, *that not a single goblin drew "The Lady"?* But she did not have long to consider this, for suddenly, standing before her, was Jack.

He looked, somehow, different.

Her eyes traveled from his messy black hair to his eyes—which seemed harder, more resolute, than she'd ever seen them before—to his set mouth, his quivering chin, his shoulders—were they broader, now?—down his thin arms and past his elbows and his wrists and to his hands . . .

She stopped.

Confused? Well, allow me to go back to Jack's story for a moment.

It was just a short while before that Jack had been standing with the dream-sword raised above his head, and his left hand outstretched on a bed of velvet.

"*Don't do it*," the frog whispered frantically. "*Jack, you will be sorry. So, so sorry.*"

Jack thought of Marie, laughing at him. He thought of his father. *It'll prove that you're a man.* He held his breath.

The blade began to sing.

This is where we left off, right?

Just checking.

———

The sword of Jack's dreams clattered to the floor.

The frog wept silently.

Neither the goblin-salesman nor the apothecary moved.

Jack looked at them, and then at the sword, and then at his hand.

He felt different. Very different.

He flexed his right hand.

Then he flexed his left.

"What happened?" said the salesman.

"You didn't do it!" the frog cried. "Hooray! Hoorah! He didn't do it!"

Jack said, "For a minute there, I felt very con-fused." He shook his head like he was waking up from a dream. Then he said, "Where's Jill?"

The goblin, trying to hide his frustration, smiled an oily smile. "Are you sure you don't want the sword? Everything you've ever wanted for will come true! Really! Really and truly!"

Jack's eyes became hazy again. But again he shook his head sharply. And then he said perhaps the wisest thing that he had ever said. He said: "Maybe I've been wanting the wrong things."

And he turned away from the goblin.

As he walked away, he said to himself, "I want Jill back."

So he went back to where he had begun and methodically

traced Jill's path. He asked questions and eavesdropped and guessed his way past the stalls of the underground market, through the tall and crooked houses of the goblin city, and finally to the shadow of an enormous, dark castle. There, Jack saw a line of goblin men, winding out of the door. He asked them what they were waiting for. He joined the line, and waited, too.

And now Jill watched Jack step forward from the line, his jaw set, his face hard. He did look different, somehow. But not in his face, nor his shoulders, nor his hands. Perhaps it was just on the inside.

Just as Jill was thinking this, Jack announced, "I want to marry the queen."

Jill screamed from within her gag. She shook her head frantically to stop him. The frog hissed madly from Jack's pocket. "Jack! She's your cousin! Is this legal? I don't think it is! And aren't you a little young to settle down? Finally, consider the fact that *they will kill you*! Jack! Jack! Are you listening to me?" But he wasn't.

Meanwhile, a thrill had run through the Goblins in the hall. "It's a human!" "There's a human!" "Is that a human?"

Two guards had stepped forward. They slammed the butts of their spears into the stone floor. "Will you risk your life to treasure and protect this lady?" the guards barked in unison.

Jack looked at Jill and smiled. "Yes. I will."

ADAM GIDWITZ

"No!" Jill wanted to cry out. "Jack! It's a trap! It's not a fair test!" All she actually said was, "*Nnnnnnjjjjjjjtttttrrrrrnnnnffrrrrrrttttttt!*"

Meanwhile, the hall exploded with sound. Goblins screamed and shouted at Jack. "She's ours!" "Leave her alone!" "No humans allowed!"

"Bring forth the casket!" the goblin guards yelled, and four other guards came forward with the great iron casket, suspended between two long poles. Again, they explained the task. "In this casket," announced the four guards in unison, "are two slips of parchment. One says 'Death!' The other says 'The Lady!' If you choose 'Death!', you will be killed right here on the spot! If you choose 'The Lady!', you will become her husband for all the rest of your days, and you and she will spend countless hours together alone, engaging in whatever pursuits give her pleasure. Do you understand?"

Jack gave a curt nod.

Jill strained against the bonds on her wrists and ankles. *No, Jack . . . No . . .*

Jack was blindfolded. Two soldiers pointed their spears into Jack's back.

The casket was brought directly before him.

Its lid was drawn back with a slow creak.

Jill watched, no longer breathing, as Jack's hand moved toward the casket's iron darkness.

"Wait."

It was Jack's voice.

"Wait," he said again. "Do you swear, on the honor of your kingdom and your queen, that this is a fair test?"

There was a pause. The great hall was deathly silent. Then one of the goblin guards, the one with the rich voice and the careworn face and the deep, old eyes, said, "It is a fair test."

"On the honor of your kingdom and your queen?" Jack pressed him.

There was another pause. Finally, Jack heard, "On the honor of the kingdom and the queen!"

Jack nodded. He slipped his hand into the chest and withdrew a piece of paper.

Jill had not drawn a breath for a good minute now. Her head felt light. She could not feel her hands or her feet.

Jack put the piece of paper in his mouth and began chewing.

For an instant, Jill had no idea what was going on.

Then the hall erupted.

"What happened?"

"What'd he do?"

"Stop him!"

These cries and more exploded from the goblin men. They clambered upon one another and pointed and howled.

Jack finished chewing the paper. He stood up and removed the blindfold.

"Well?" he said, swallowing the last pulpy pieces. "Which one did I choose?"

The goblin guards stared at him, gaping. The frog stood up in Jack's pocket and shouted, "How do we know? You ate it, you idiot!"

"Well," Jack replied, making his voice loud enough that everyone in the hall could hear it, "why don't you check what's in the casket now? If the remaining piece of parchment says 'The Lady!', then clearly I chose 'Death!'. If, on the other hand, the remaining piece says "Death!", I must have chosen 'The Lady!'"

There was another moment of silence in the hall, and then, from within her gag, Jill began to laugh.

She couldn't help it. She laughed and laughed and kept laughing.

The goblin with the deep eyes and the careworn face was saying, "You see . . . well . . . it's not strictly . . ."

But the other goblins clamored, "He's right!" "It's common sense!" "What's the other piece of paper say?"

The goblin with the deep eyes glanced worriedly out at them, and then cast a dark look at Jack. He walked up, reached into the casket, and held the paper aloft. He closed his eyes as if he were very angry with himself and said quietly, "It reads, 'Death!'"

A roar went up from the goblins in the hall. They shouted angry imprecations at Jack, cursed their own luck for arriving too late, damned the goblin with the deep voice for allowing a human to take their queen. They were so angry you could have colored each goblin's face with that green that the crayon company makes, and you would have gotten it just about right.

Jack sprung up onto the throne and removed Jill's gag from her mouth. She was grinning. "You crazy fool," she said. He ripped the silken cords from her ankles and wrists, and she threw herself into his arms.

And then they turned around. Twenty goblins guards with glistering spears were arrayed in a circle around them. In the center stood the goblin with the careworn face, the rich voice, and the deep, old eyes. He did not look happy.

CHAPTER NINE

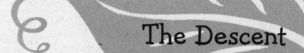

The Descent

Once upon a time, a boy named Jack and a girl named Jill landed roughly on the stone floor of a small room.

Goblin guards swarmed into the room behind them, followed by the goblin with the old eyes. He walked slowly. It looked as if he always walked that way, as if there were nothing in the world that could make him hurry, nothing in the world that worried him, nothing in the world that those old eyes had not seen.

"Clever." His rich voice reverberated through the small room. "I was outwitted. Begehren is not often outwitted."

Jack and Jill pulled themselves to their knees. Jill squinted balefully up at the goblin.

His uniform was the same as any of the goblin guards'. But the age and wisdom in his face made him look as much like the other guards as a swan does a duck.

"Nor do I enjoy it," he added. "So tell me, and tell me swiftly: What is it you want?"

Jill pulled herself to her feet. "We want the Seeing Glass," she said.

The goblin Begehren started as if he'd been hit in the gut. He said, "The what . . . ?"

"The Seeing Glass."

Around the walls of the room, the goblin guards began muttering to one another. Begehren rubbed his hands together. He muttered, "You do, do you? The Seeing Glass . . ."

"Do you know where it is?" Jack demanded.

Jill said, "Of course he does . . . just look at him."

Begehren stared into the middle distance. Then, quite suddenly, he roused himself. "What? Oh, yes. The Seeing Glass. I know where it is. But no one has sought the Glass for a thousand years." His deep eyes scoured their faces. "How do you know of it?"

Jack hesitated. But Jill said, "We swore we'd find it. We swore on our very lives."

The goblin smiled. "Ah. But to whom did you swear?"

"An old lady," said Jill.

"A crazy old lady," added Jack.

Begehren's eyes narrowed. "She didn't happen to have pale blue eyes and a face eerily like a babe's, did she?"

Jack and Jill nodded warily.

"Ah." Begehren smiled. "The Others have come to your kingdom. Too bad for you. And how," he asked, "are you supposed to carry the Glass back to this 'crazy old lady'?"

"What do you mean," said Jack. "Is it . . . very heavy or something?"

"Is it heavy?!" The goblin laughed. "It is the greatest treasure horde in the history of the world!"

Both children now started as if *they* had been hit in the gut.

The goblin's eyes glazed over as he spoke: "It is a treasure so great a king could trade his kingdom for it and be counted a wise man. The ancient writings say that the sun becomes dim when the shining face of its riches is revealed to the sky. Pilgrims would travel the world over just to look at it. It was the pride, the guide, the purpose of the Goblin Kingdom.

"You see, the golden age of the Goblin Kingdom lasted a thousand years," Begehren went on, and his voice was deep and rich as polished wood. "We were ruled by wise, errorless sages. And they made every decision by consulting the Seeing Glass."

Jack was about ask, *How do you consult a treasure?*, but Jill hushed him.

"They consulted the Seeing Glass, and, as wise as it was valuable, it always told them the truth. It was, as I said, a golden age. But alas," the goblin continued, "we live now in an age of error; we see, not with the Glass, but dimly. For there came a day, one horrible, dark day, when something evil erupted from the belly of the earth. It was massive and vicious—a beast unlike anything ever seen before. It sought to lay waste to our kingdom. We arrayed our vast armies against it and gave our lives to defend the kingdom—and our Glass.

"The tales that survive from those days of war, when the fate of the goblin people was in flux, are our greatest epics, and our greatest tragedies. For in the end, though our soldiers fought to the very death, they were no match for the beast from the center of the earth. For the Eidechse von Feuer, der Menschenfleischfressende."

"The what?" said Jack.

"The Eidechse von Feuer, der Menschenfleischfressende," the goblin repeated.

You want to say that word, don't you? How could you not? I mean, come on. It's like thirteen syllables.

———

Here's how:

I-DECK-SUH VON FOY-ER, DARE MEN-SHEN FLYSH-FRESS-ENDUH.

See? That wasn't so bad.

Now, I expect you to say it every time I write it, because it takes a minute and a half to type it out, and if I'm going to all that trouble, you'd better, too.

"What's does it mean?" asked Jack.

"Well," replied Begehren, "it's the beast's name. But, roughly translated, Eidechse von Feuer, der Menschenfleischfressende means something like, 'Lizard-that-is-made-of-fire-and-eats-human-flesh.'"

"Oh," said Jack. "Of course."

"The Eidechse von Feuer, der Menschenfleischfressende was invincible. Made of bone and fire, he never once, in all the great battles the goblins waged against him, was so much as injured." Begehren's deep eyes seemed to cloud over with memories, as if he had himself seen that horrible war, a thousand years ago. Perhaps he had. "He kills reflexively, as if he were born to. Were he even to breathe in your direction, you would be burned to a cinder. He is as cruel and perfect a killing machine as has ever lived.

"Eidechse von Feuer, der Menschenfleischfressende took the Seeing Glass from us, and withdrew with it to his lair in the belly of the earth. Our kings were dead. Our heroes defeated. Now it is left to me, inadequate as I am, to care for the kingdom until the Glass is recovered, and our sage-kings and heroes return."

Jack and Jill felt almost sorry for him.

Begehren was staring at them. With his goblin-green fingers, he played thoughtfully with a single long hair that grew from the end of his chin.

"But you," he said, "you two are sworn to get the Seeing Glass."

Jack and Jill hesitated.

"On your lives, you said."

The frog began to quiver.

"Well," Begehren announced, suddenly grinning, "what are you waiting for?"

They traveled in something like a carriage. It was golden and royal and very luxurious. But, like all very luxurious things, it had much in common with a cage. Jill stared through silver bars at the dark, winding alleyways of the Goblin Kingdom. Cobblestone streets twisted out of sight, and buildings of four stories hung out over the little alleys crazily.

Jack said, "I don't get it. Is it a treasure or a mirror?"

Jill shrugged. "Maybe it's both."

"What does that mean? It's a giant mirror of gold or something?"

Jill shrugged again.

"What does it matter?" the frog moaned. "We're going to be murdered by this I-deck-suh-whatever as soon as we get down there anyway."

"That's true," said Jill.

Jack was watching the Goblin Kingdom go by. "You know that deal we made with the old lady?" he said at last. "I don't think it was a good one."

In the center of the Goblin Kingdom was a great sinkhole. It was protected by a thick iron fence. Forged into the iron were intricate images of a terrible beast blowing fire and destroying a kingdom and devouring goblins. All around the iron fence, staring darkly at Jack and Jill, were dozens and dozens of soldiers.

Begehren stood before a heavily padlocked gate. He followed the children with his deep, old, black eyes. "Give them weapons!" he called. Two goblin guards stepped forward and handed Jack and Jill spears.

"Thanks," said the frog. "Those'll do a lot of good."

Begehren moved to the iron gate and unlocked it with a twisted, ancient key. A soldier led Jack and Jill to the edge of the sinkhole. Heat radiated up from it. Next to the sinkhole there stood a giant bucket, attached to a long rope. Jack and Jill were told to get into the bucket. Once they had, four goblin guards lifted the bucket and held it, and the children, too, out over the darkness.

Begehren said to Jack and Jill, "Are you ready?"

Jill was about to shake her head.

Jack was about to ask, "How far down is it?"

The frog was about to scream at the top of his lungs.

But suddenly, their stomachs jolted into their throats and tried to squeeze out of their mouths. Jill's hair was standing straight up on her head. The frog was upside down in the air, gripping Jack's shirt with his froggy hands. They were falling.

They fell and fell and fell and kept falling.

And then, suddenly, the bucket stopped in midair, and the frog plunged back into Jack's pocket and the two children slammed into the bottom of the bucket.

They shook themselves. They raised themselves to their feet in the great bucket. Jack said, "Frog, did you just throw up in my pocket?"

The frog poked his head up woozily. "Can I go in Jill's pocket now?" he moaned. "This one smells."

"Absolutely not," said Jill.

They hung in near-blackness. The only light was the glow from the fires in the Goblin Kingdom way up above their heads, and an eerie phosphorescence on the rocks all around them. The long rope swung slightly back and forth, back and forth, creaking. Jack peered over the edge of the bucket. There was no sign of a bottom to the sinkhole.

Again, the bucket began to descend. But slowly.

And then, they heard a voice. "How will they get the treasure back up?"

Jill looked all around her. Jack gripped the edge of the bucket.

"Who said that?" the frog whispered.

"They'll just hoist it up, piece by piece," said another voice. It sounded like Begehren. But they could hear it as if he were right next to them.

"But if the treasure's anything like what the legends say, that could take a lifetime!" Jack and Jill stared at the glowing walls, passing slowly by. The voices seemed to be ringing through the stone.

"If it takes a lifetime, it takes a lifetime. What's another eighty years," said Begehren, "after the thousand we have waited?"

Jack and Jill looked at each other, their eyes wide.

"But they won't get it, right?" asked the voice. "They'll be killed."

"One way or another," Begehren replied. "Almost certainly by the Eidechse von Feuer, die Meschenfleischfressende. And if not, once they hand over the Glass, we won't need them anymore. So I'll kill them myself."

Jack went pale.

"I like him less and less," whispered Jill.

The frog began to weep.

The bucket descended farther and farther into the impenetrable gloom, and beads of sweat began to stand out on Jack's and Jill's foreheads, faces, necks, arms. Farther, farther, farther. With every few yards the children descended, the heat climbed another degree. The air was so thick they could barely breathe. It was as if they were being lowered into a forge, as if the children were metal, and they would melt and re-form themselves in the heat of the sinkhole. At least, those were the strange thoughts that passed through Jack's head as he gasped for breath. Jill was so hot she could not think of anything at all. And the frog was still weeping.

At last, the bucket landed with a bump on a craggy outcropping of stone. The children crawled out. There was no relief from the heat. The spears, which had been jarred from their hands when the bucket stopped suddenly in midair, lay on the black rock. One was shattered to pieces.

210

"Great," said Jack.

"Oh, because it would have helped," said the frog.

Jill said, "Where do we go now?"

There was a small, dark tunnel that led away from the outcropping where they had landed. Jack pointed to it. Jill scanned the rest of the walls for any other passageways or doors. There were none. "Okay," she said.

"Yeah," said the frog. "Fantastic."

So Jack scooped up the remaining spear, took Jill's hand, and they walked into the dark, narrow, oppressively hot tunnel. Here, too, the rock glowed with that eerie phosphorescence. All it allowed the children to see, though, was that the tunnel was dark and rocky and descended gradually toward the center of the earth.

The children walked in silence, thinking about what Begehren had told them of the beast. *He kills reflexively, as if he were born to. Were he even to breathe in your direction, you would be burned to a cinder. He is as cruel and perfect a killing machine as has ever lived.* And they thought of all that they had heard of the Glass. *It is a treasure horde so great a king could trade his kingdom for it and be counted a wise man . . . The greatest power, it is said, resides in that Glass . . . If you can't find it, you die.*

Deeper and deeper, deeper and deeper into the darkness. The children stopped and tried to catch their breath. Even walking in this heat was a trial. Deeper and deeper. Hotter and hotter.

"I may be turning into a casserole," the frog muttered.

Deeper.

Hotter.

Deeper.

Sweat poured off the children's faces. They could barely breathe for the heat.

The frog was now praying.

The dark tunnel continued down, down, down. The heat wrapped them in a bear hug and squeezed their lungs. But the heat was not the only thing that intensified. It began with Jill sniffing and wrinkling her nose. Then Jack said, "What *is* that?" Soon, the children—and the frog—were covering their noses and mouths, trying not to breathe because of the horrible, putrefying stench. It was as if flesh were rotting, had been rotting, for a thousand years. Jack bent over, put his hand on the pockmarked black wall, and tried not to be sick. He gagged and held his throat. At last, he straightened up, and the children staggered on.

They became dizzier and dizzier with the heat and the smell. *How will we fight this thing?* Jack thought. *I can barely walk. I can barely see straight.* He would have said as much to Jill, but he didn't want to open his mouth, for fear of the pungent funk. And besides, he didn't need to, because Jill was wondering the same thing.

The tunnel became narrower, and narrower, and narrower,

until Jack and Jill were crouching, and then crawling. Their shirts, their hair, their socks were soaked with sweat.

The rock beneath them became hotter, until the sweat that ran off of their faces sizzled as it landed on the black stone. The palms of their hands were burning.

The tunnel turned precipitously. The frog, peering out of Jack's pocket, said, "Holy . . ."

Jack looked up. "Have mercy . . ." he muttered.

Jill came up behind them. She opened her mouth. No sound came out at all.

CHAPTER TEN

Eidechse von Feuer, Der Menschenfleischfressende

Once upon a time, there was a huge cavern under the earth.

Jack and Jill and the frog stared.

But the cavern was not what they were staring at.

At the back of the cavern, a torrent of lava poured out of a rock wall, red and black and lurid and glowing.

But that was not what they were staring at, either.

The torrent tumbled into a magma river that wound its way around the back of the cavern, hugging the pockmarked black wall closely and then, in the distance, feeding into an endless underground lava sea.

But the three travelers were also not staring at that.

They were staring at a small mountain that sat beside the

winding lava river. The mountain was made not of rock, nor of magma, but of pink, fleshy skin. The mountain had a ridge like a backbone, and little valleys formed by small arms and legs, and a slope of a wide, flat tail. There was no head. But its body rose and fell with breath. They could see thin black bones through the pink skin, and in the distended bag of a belly, black organs wound around one another, pulsing.

"I don't want to do this . . ." Jill whispered.

Jack shook his head and muttered, "Maybe we can go back and beg Begehren to let us up."

"Or we can just live down here . . ."

The two children backed into the tunnel they'd come from as swiftly as they could.

But the frog said, "Wait."

"*What?*" hissed Jill.

"What?" said Jack, a little louder than he'd intended to.

Jill looked at Jack, eyes wide, finger before her lips. Jack slapped his hand over his mouth.

Silence.

Jack said a wordless prayer of thanks.

And then there was a roar. A roar that has never been described accurately, in all the times this tale has been told. A roar that shook the walls and the roof, that caused waves in the lava sea, that made Jack and Jill fear their eardrums would burst,

ADAM GIDWITZ

that made their very bones vibrate and ache within their bodies, that was felt in a tremble not only up in the Goblin Kingdom, but indeed, even on the surface of the earth above that. Jack and Jill fell back into the tunnel, covering their ears and burying their heads between their knees and wishing, wishing, wishing the sound would stop.

And then there was heat. It scorched the children's faces and arms, turning their skin red and blistery in an instant. Flame followed the heat, and it rolled up against their little tunnel like a beast that was too big to chase them any farther. The flame was red and yellow and blue and pale green, and Jack and Jill would have thought it was one of the most magnificent things they had ever seen in their lives—if their heads hadn't been clamped firmly between their knees.

Finally, the flame subsided. The children peeked out from their protective positions. The frog had fallen from Jack's pocket and was curled in a ball on the ground.

The children leaped to their feet. "GO!" Jack cried.

But the frog cried, "Wait!"

Jill hesitated, but Jack was already sprinting away, his spear discarded, his arms flailing wildly as he ran. "Wait!" said the frog again. "He only wants to know who we are!"

Halfway down the hall, Jack slowed to a jog.

"Excuse me?" said Jill.

"He was asking who we are," said the frog.

Jill was staring at the frog in an attempt to determine if he had lost his mind. Jack had very much the same look on his face.

"He speaks Amphibian," said the frog, and shrugged his little froggy shoulders.

"You're joking . . ." said Jack.

"You're certain?" said Jill.

"Sure," said the frog. "It's my language."

The floor began to shake, the air heated to boiling, and Jack and Jill clamped their hands over their ears as another roar rocked the tunnel, the cavern, and the earth miles and miles above.

When it had subsided, Jill asked the frog, "Well? Was that Amphibian, too?"

"Yeah," said the frog. "He wants to know where we went."

Jack started laughing hysterically, and Jill was pretty sure that both of her companions had suddenly lost their minds.

"Let's go talk to him," said the frog. Jack continued to laugh insanely.

Jill looked back and forth between the two and, since Jack wasn't giving her any better options, she followed the frog back to the very edge of the cavern.

The mountain had moved. It had turned and raised a humongous, grotesque, fleshy, pink head. This head was roughly the size of the rest of its body, excluding its long, thick tail. It had tiny black eyes that sat where you might have expected ears to be, just above the upward curves at the end of its wide mouth.

"Oh boy," said the frog.

"What?" Jill whispered.

"It's a salamander."

Jill stared. "It is?"

The frog nodded.

"Is that bad?" Jill asked.

The frog shrugged. "Well, they're not terribly clever."

The mountainous salamander stared at them out of the tiny black eyes on either side of his head.

"I'm going to introduce us," the frog said. Jill nodded as if this made sense. Jack walked up to them, giggling and mumbling about all the king's horses and all the king's men putting his head back together again. Then he tried to make his elbow touch his nose.

The frog croaked again. The beast opened his mouth, revealing a big pink tongue. Then out poured a roar that seemed to never end. Jill curled up in a ball and covered her ears. She thought they might be bleeding.

"He says his name is Eidechse von Feuer, der Menschen-fleischfressende," said the frog.

"Yeah," said Jill, "we figured." Then she said, "Can you ask him not to talk so loud? I think I'm going deaf."

"Sure," said the frog. So he croaked at Eidechse von Feuer, der Menschenfleischfressende. The giant salamander roared a roar that hurt Jill's ears and blew her hair back but did not force her to curl up into a ball and want to die.

"Better," she mumbled.

"He said his name is Eidechse von Feuer, der Menschenfleischfressende again."

"Yeah," said Jill. "We got it." Jack giggled and tried to fit his fist into his mouth.

"Also," added the frog, "he said he prefers to be called Eddie."

Jill was about to say something and then realized that there was absolutely nothing to say to that.

The frog croaked some more. "Eddie" roared back. "I just introduced you two," said the frog. "He wants to know what's wrong with Jack." Eidechse von Feuer, der Menschenfleischfressende's head was held alertly up, and he seemed to be studying Jack curiously with his tiny black eyes. Jill turned around to see Jack trying to fit his left leg over his head.

Jill took him by the shoulders and shook him. Then she slapped him across the face. He shook himself. He said, "What happened? Where am I?"

Jill pointed to Eidechse von Feuer, der Menschenfleischfressende. "He's a salamander. His name's Eddie."

Jack started to giggle again, so Jill slapped him across the face again. Again Jack shook himself. "Sorry. What?" He looked up. "Oh." And then, again, he said, "Oh."

The children stared up at the beast of the translucent skin and the putrid odor. After a moment, Jill said, "Well, I guess we should ask him about the Glass?"

The frog said, "Right. Good idea." So he croaked up at Eddie. The salamander roared.

"He apologizes," said the frog. "Apparently he ate it."

"He *ate* the *treasure*?" Jill exclaimed.

"Oh, boy," said Jack.

The salamander reared back with his huge, pink, fleshy head and roared some more. "He's very sorry," said the frog. "He didn't mean to."

"At least he's polite . . ." Jack marveled.

"He said someone dropped it into his pit a long time ago by accident, and he ate it."

"Can you—" Jill began, but the frog cut her off.

"Sure," he said. "I'll ask him to explain."

So the frog croaked at the salamander. The salamander wrapped his enormous, fleshy tail around his legs. As he moved it, the cavern shook and shifted, and in the distance hundreds of stone stalactites fell from the rock ceiling into the lava sea. The salamander roared.

"He says he didn't used to live so far under the ground," said the frog. "He used to live near the surface."

The salamander roared again. "The goblins used to like him, he says. He sounds kind of sad about it."

The salamander roared yet again. "He powered their forges with his breath." The frog waited for more from the salamander.

When there'd been silence for a moment too long, the frog croaked at him.

Eddie roared in reply.

The frog said to the children, "Right. Sorry. He's starting the story over again. You've got to get used to this with salamanders. It's very hard for them to remember anything they've said more than a few sentences ago."

After a bit of roaring, the frog said, "Okay, he's back to where we left off. So he lived in a big sinkhole, and would breathe fire to heat the goblins' homes and power their forges. But then, one day, at some ceremony that he tried to explain but I didn't understand, they dropped the Glass into his mouth. By accident. And they were very mad." Jack and Jill looked up at the salamander. He was watching them with his tiny black eyes, as if he wished they would understand.

The frog croaked at Eddie, and Eddie roared some more. "He forgot where he was again. Hold on." The frog croaked, the salamander roared, and the frog turned to Jack and Jill. "And we're back. So once he'd swallowed their treasure, they drove him deep down into the earth by dropping boulders on his head and pouring cold water on him, which he did not like at all. So now he lives down here by himself, and he never gets to ask anyone any questions."

"He never gets to what?" said Jill.

"Ask anyone any questions," replied the frog. "You know. Salamanders love to ask stupid questions."

"Oh," said Jack and Jill at once. "Right."

They stood there in silence, staring up at the massive, grotesque head of the beast, who stared back down at them as if he was waiting for something.

The frog said, "Hold on," and he began croaking at the salamander. The salamander nodded his huge head and the whole cavern shook. "It's still in his stomach!" said the frog. "It's lodged right next to his intestines. He can feel it!"

Jill thought she was going to be sick. Jack said, "You mean, he could cough it up for us?"

The frog croaked at Eddie. Eddie roared back.

"He's tried to disgorge it for however many hundreds of years he's had it in there. He can't. But he'd be happy to let you go in and get it." Jill turned green and shook her head violently.

Eddie's tiny eyes narrowed. Jack looked up at him and thought that that was probably what passed for a sly look for a salamander. Eddie roared. The frog turned to the children. "But before he lets you crawl down his throat, we have to answer his questions."

"That doesn't sound so bad," said Jack.

"It's going to be awful," said the frog.

"Can we go back to the part about 'crawling down his throat'?" Jill interjected.

"One trauma at a time, please," said the frog. He croaked at Eddie, and was answered by a roar. The frog smiled. He turned to Jack and Jill. "What's better, red or blue?" he said.

"What?" said Jack.

"Is that a joke?" said Jill.

The frog smiled smugly at them. "It's the first question. Welcome to my world."

"I don't know!" said Jill. "What's the right answer?"

"No idea," said the frog. "That's the beauty of it."

"Blue," said Jack.

"Red," said Jill.

Eddie roared loudly. Jack and Jill clamped their hands over their ears. "Don't confuse him," said the frog. He turned and croaked at Eddie.

"What'd you say?" Jill demanded.

"Purple," replied the frog. "Compromise."

"He accepted that?" asked Jack. But Eddie's eyes were glazed over and his mouth was drawn back like he was lost in a contemplative smile.

"That's going to be a lot of information for him to process," said the frog. "Give him a minute now." Sure enough, a few minutes passed, and the salamander stopped grinning and roared again. "He wants to know which is bigger, the sky or the earth."

"The sky," said Jill.

"The earth," said Jack.

Eddie roared, and Jack and Jill covered their ears. Their bones shook. "Guys!" the frog hissed.

Jill whispered, "The sky goes all the way around the earth, and it is really, really high! It's bigger!"

"But the earth is really thick," replied Jack. "It's like wrapping a ball in a quilt! Which is bigger, the ball or the quilt?"

"Depends on the quilt," said Jill.

The frog turned and croaked.

"What'd you tell him?" Jill wanted to know.

"Yes," said the frog.

"What's that supposed to mean?"

The frog glanced up at the mountainous salamander. "I'm not sure. But he's working on it." Eddie's eyes were rolled back in his head, as if he were trying to remember what question he'd asked, and if yes was an acceptable answer. Eventually he seemed to decide that it was. He roared again.

"He says he's always wanted to know which was hotter, summer or winter."

Jill smacked her forehead. "How long is this going to go on?"

"Just answer him," Jack told the frog. So the frog did. The salamander shook the cavern with his appreciative nodding. He roared again.

"He wants to know if smelly is good or smelly is bad."

Jack and Jill laughed out loud at that. The salamander roared fiercely, and a ball of fire exploded from his mouth. They both stopped laughing.

"Bad," said Jill.

"Right," said Jack.

"Wrong," said the frog, and he turned and croaked at Eddie. Eddie seemed very, very happy. He roared another question.

"He says, 'Am I smelly? Very smelly? How smelly?'"

"Very smelly," both children said at once. Jill added, "Unbelievably smelly."

The frog turned and croaked at Eddie, and Eddie's head started bobbing up and down, up and down. "He's very excited," said the frog. Eddie asked another question.

"Does everyone have a birthday?" the frog relayed to the children.

Jill hesitated. But Jack said, "Yes," and the frog told Eddie. Eddie roared.

"He wants to know when his is," said the frog.

The children looked at each other and raised their eyebrows. "What should we say?" Jack asked the frog quietly. The frog shrugged.

"Say yesterday," said Jill. "And tell him we're sorry we missed it, but congratulations anyway." The frog turned and croaked that to Eddie, who looked a little deflated, but appreciative of their belated good wishes. He roared.

"Are salamanders people, too?" said the frog to Jack and Jill.

Jill looked at Eddie, with his grotesque translucent skin, his hideously wide mouth, his distended belly, and his thick, fleshy tail. But then she looked at his little black eyes, set just where you'd expect his ears to be. They looked at her. "Of course," she said, and she smiled at him. Jack nodded vigorously in agreement.

So Eddie started nodding, too. He nodded so hard that the ground shook up and down and knocked Jack and Jill over. Then Eddie lay his head down on the ground and smiled.

All of a sudden, Jill did something that surprised her as much as it surprised everyone else. She got up and walked slowly toward Eddie. When she was just a few feet from his enormous, horrible-smelling head, she reached out and she touched it. It was slimy and fleshy and diaphanous enough to see his skull bones through it. She let her hand come to rest on his nose.

Jack scooped up the frog and followed Jill. He, too, rested his hand on Eddie's nose. The giant salamander sighed, and Jack and Jill and the frog were enveloped in the foulest stench you can imagine. And they laughed.

The frog said, "Well, shall we get the Glass?"

Jack and Jill nodded. So the frog croaked at the salamander.

Eddie opened his mouth.

"That," said the frog, "looks like an invitation."

Eddie's mouth was probably eight feet across and six feet tall when open. Near the front were a row of small teeth—well, small for Eddie. Each was about six inches high and shaped like a little triangle. After the row of teeth there was a patch of pink flesh, and then, about a foot farther back, was another row of slightly larger teeth. Behind the second row of teeth was an enormous mound of a tongue. Farther back was a wide, dark passage that led down Eddie's throat. It all looked pretty gross, of course. But how it looked was nothing compared to how it smelled.

Jill spun away as soon as Eddie opened his mouth. But Jack just clamped his hand over his nose and said to the frog, "Please don't let him close it while we're in there."

"What about the fire?" Jill asked, still facing the other direction.

The frog croaked and Eddie closed his mouth and roared. "He won't burn you," said the frog. "Unless he burps."

"Do salamanders burp often?"

"All the time," replied the frog.

Jill sighed. "Remind him to keep his mouth open." The frog croaked some more. Eddie nodded with his mouth open.

Jill turned back toward Eddie, closed her eyes, did not take a deep breath, and grabbed Jack's left hand. But Jack said, "Wait." He ran back into the corridor and got his discarded spear. While it was not necessarily hospitable to take a weapon into someone's gastrointestinal tract, Jack certainly wasn't going in there without it.

The children stepped over Eddie's lip and into his mouth.

The frog quietly croaked at Eddie, reminding him not to close his mouth and not to breathe any fire and to try, try, try not to burp.

"We could die right now," said Jack.

"I trust Eddie," said Jill.

"Then you're probably as dumb as he is," Jack replied. But he didn't mean it. He was just a little tense.

Hand in hand, they stepped over the first row of teeth, and then the second. Jill reached out with her foot and touched Eddie's tongue. It shivered and then lay still. She looked over her shoulder at the frog. The frog nodded at her and kept up his constant stream of reminders to Eddie. Jill stepped onto Eddie's tongue. It did not move. Jack followed her. They walked across the tongue. The stench became worse, the air thicker and hotter. Jill gagged.

"Don't," Jack said severely. Jill swallowed hard.

They approached the dark hole of Eddie's throat. "Ready?" said Jack.

Together, they ducked through the giant aperture and into the blackness of Eddie's esophagus.

A rumble came from Eddie's belly. Jack and Jill froze and gripped each other's hand more tightly. They could hear the frog croaking.

"Why do we have to do this?" said Jack quietly. "Why are we bothering?"

"Greatest treasure in the history of the world. Very powerful. We don't get it, we die," Jill answered.

"Right. Just wanted to make sure this wasn't optional or anything."

"Not optional."

The esophagus narrowed, and Jack and Jill were forced to crawl, their hands and knees sliding along his slimy throat. The growling grew louder. And then it was joined by a buzzing.

"What's that?"

Jill was slapped in the face by an enormous bug. She frantically swatted it away. Another one crashed into Jack's neck. Jack screamed and then shuddered.

They pushed on. The darkness became heavier.

"Look for treasure. Or a giant mirror," Jack whispered. Jill nodded.

The two children slid out of the esophagus and into the stomach. This was a burbling swamp of acid that burned their skin when they touched it. Foul-smelling gloop dripped from the ceiling and coated their bodies and then began to sting. Jack and Jill winced in pain. They couldn't hear the frog any more. "Hurry," said Jill. They pushed deeper. Bugs slapped them in the face and got caught in the sticky, stinging gloop. The children pulled them off, and the bugs protested and stung at their hands. Jill thought she might cry. But she gasped, "Deeper."

On they pushed. They felt with their feet under the pool of acid for treasure chests or strings of pearls or golden mirrors. Anything that might be the Seeing Glass.

They found nothing.

"It's not here," Jack said.

"Maybe Eddie got mixed up."

"Maybe he digested it."

"I can't believe it's not here."

Sudden panic gripped the children. "What are we going to do now?" Jack demanded.

They arrived at the back of Eddie's stomach. There, in the dim light that filtered from Eddie's mouth and down his throat, they could make out a round little hatch of muscle. It led, they figured, to his intestines.

"That's all there is," said Jack. "The end."

But suddenly Jill was pointing at something.

It did not look like a bug, or like anything edible.

It was a round disc, about a foot in diameter.

"What's that?" Jill asked. They waded up to it. It was lodged in the hatch of muscle.

ADAM GIDWITZ

"Dunno," said Jack.

"Pull it out."

"If I do it I think I'm going to throw up."

"Well, I *know* I will," said Jill.

So Jack grabbed hold of the little disc that was lodged between Eddie's stomach and intestines and yanked at it. It came out easily, and Jack fell backward into the burbling stomach acid. The acid burned his skin. He shouted and scrambled to his feet.

Suddenly, everything went black. Eddie's entire stomach began to shift, and Jack and Jill were thrown into the fleshy back wall. Eddie was rearing up. Stomach acid poured all over the children, burning their faces, their arms, their hands, submerging them utterly. Jill began swimming upward to get to air, but Jack, holding onto the little disc with one hand and the spear with the other, could not. Jill reached the surface, looked for Jack, and began to scream. Suddenly, Eddie slammed back to the ground, sending Jack crashing into Jill, and both sprawling into the stomach acid again.

They got to their feet and groped frantically through the pitch darkness toward the throat.

"What's going on?" Jill asked, terrified.

"No idea. He forgot?"

"Or he's decided to eat us?"

"Was it a trap?"

And then the darkness was cut by an orange glow. Jack and Jill looked in the direction of Eddie's mouth. It was still tightly shut, and no light came through at all. Where was the glow coming from, then? They looked back into the stomach. A small fire was burning there at the back. A small fire. But growing.

"He's erupting!" Jill shouted, and though that wasn't exactly the word she was looking for at that moment, it was in fact exactly the right word. For the fire was blooming up the length of Eddie's stomach. Jack thrust the disc to Jill and gripped the spear with both hands.

"What are you going to do?" Jill screamed.

"I don't know!"

The fire boiled toward them.

"This way!" Jill shouted, and she grabbed Jack's arm and they crawled through the esophagus and into Eddie's mouth.

"Eddie, open up! Open up!" she cried. Something exploded in Eddie's stomach. The fire burst into Eddie's throat. Jack aimed the spear at the roof of Eddie's mouth.

"You're going to kill him!" Jill shouted.

"What else can I do?" Jack cried.

"EDDIE!" Jill screamed.

And Jack sent the spear straight up at the soft part of Eddie's palate.

And then, just before the point of Jack's spear hit Eddie's flesh, the giant mouth opened and the great tongue flung Jill and Jack and Jack's spear out of Eddie's mouth. They spun through the air and hit the ground hard as an arm of flame burst from Eddie's throat and cut a line through the air just above the children's bodies.

The flame died. Jack and Jill turned and looked at Eddie. He roared.

"Good God!" the frog cried.

Eddie kept roaring.

"What happened?" Jack and Jill shouted at the same moment.

"He had to burp," said the frog. "I kept telling him not to. Eventually he closed his mouth to keep the burp down."

"Why didn't you call to us?" Jack demanded.

"I did! You didn't hear me?"

The children shook their heads.

"What's all over you?" the frog said. Jack and Jill looked at their arms, hands, bodies. They touched their faces. Their skin was raw and blistering, and totally covered in stomach acid. "You look horrible," the frog added.

"Thanks," Jill replied.

"And no treasure?"

Jack held up the little disc. "This is all we could find." The frog turned and croaked at Eddie. Eddie nodded and roared.

"That's it," said the frog.

"What? That's the whole treasure?"

"According to him," the frog shrugged.

Jill, still lying on the ground, let her head fall against the craggy black stone. Jack stared at the disc. It was so coated in stomach gloop he couldn't make it out. "What is it?" he said. No one answered.

Jack sat up, cradled the thing in his lap, and pawed at the gloop with his fingers. It stung them. He pulled at it, but it just drooped back into place, hugging the little disc.

"Maybe it's a mirror," Jack concluded.

"We better hope so," agreed Jill.

Eddie roared. Jill looked up wearily at the giant, ecstatic salamander. "What is he saying?" she asked.

The frog sighed. "He wants to ask us more questions."

Some hours passed while the children recuperated from their ordeal and fielded such questions as, "If a tree falls in a forest and there's nobody around, how did it fall down?" and "What does the word 'is' mean?" But finally Jack stood up and said, "I think we should go now." Jill, who had been coming up with the bulk of the answers to Eddie's questions, gratefully agreed.

"The problem is," said Jack, "there's no way Begehren is going to believe that this thing is all the treasure that's down here." He waved the disc in the air. The gloop was beginning to harden. "How are we going to get him to lift us back up?"

The frog offered a suggestion, and then Jill did, and then Jack came up with one of his own. None seemed particularly promising. Jill tried another, and another. Jack added to one, subtracted from the other. The frog offered a variant. After a while, the two children were nodding.

"That might work," said Jill.

"It's the best we've got," said Jack. "Let's try it."

Jill turned to the frog. "Tell Eddie."

When the frog informed Eddie of their intent to leave, Eddie was crestfallen. But when the frog elaborated that they would need the giant salamander's help, he looked like it might be the very best day of his long, long life.

"Tell him to lead the way," Jack said to the frog. So Eddie began crashing through the tunnels that had led them there, smashing stone as easily as one might smash glass. Jack and Jill ran after him, the frog nestled in Jack's pocket.

———

Jack and Jill stood at the bottom of the sinkhole and stared up. Far above, they could see the dim red light of the Goblin Kingdom. Beside them lay Eddie, still as death. Jack nodded at Jill. They cupped their hands to their mouths and shouted, "Begehren!"

Their voices echoed up the sides of the sinkhole and then died away.

No answer came.

Jill nodded at Jack. Again they cupped their hands to their mouths and shouted, "BEGEHREN!"

Again, no answer.

A third time they cupped their hands to their mouths, turned them to the great hole, and bellowed.

This time, far up above, a tiny round shape appeared, framed by the dim red light. "QUEEN? JACK?" called a voice. It ricocheted off the walls of the sinkhole all the way down into the ground.

"YES!" the children shouted. "WE GOT IT!"

Their answer was met by a burst of sound. Excited voices seemed to be calling out to one another. Then they heard, "Begehren is coming!"

A few minutes later, another round shape appeared in the dim red light far above the two children. "DO YOU HAVE IT?"

The caretaker of the Goblin Kingdom's deep voice echoed down into the hole.

"YES!" the children called back.

The large bucket came plunging down through the darkness and landed with a crash beside them. "START LOADING IT IN!" Begehren cried down.

"WE CAN'T!" the children shouted back up. "IT'S IN THE IDECKWHATEVER'S STOMACH! WE KILLED HIM AND LOOKED IN HIS MOUTH. IT'S ALL SOLID INSIDE!"

Begehren cried, "YOU KILLED HIM????"

"IT WASN'T VERY HARD! HE WAS SLEEPING!"

There were cries of surprise and joy above.

"WHAT'S IN HIS STOMACH? GOLD? DIAMONDS?"

"YES!" the children called. "AND MORE! MUCH MORE THAN THAT! ALL IN ONE GREAT BALL!"

Shrieking laughter echoed down the hole.

"WE'LL NEED A BIG PLATFORM," Jill cried up. "YOU CAN LOAD HIM ONTO IT AND HAUL HIM UP. WE'LL COME UP AFTER."

"YES, YES, GOOD!" Begehren called down. "JUST WAIT WHILE WE GET IT!" More shrieking laughter and giddy voices. Begehren's voice returned. "YOU ARE THE GREATEST

HEROES KNOWN TO GOBLIN OR TO MAN!" And then he shouted, "HOLD ON!"

They waited, and waited, and then down through the darkness came an enormous platform with three dozen of the strongest goblins the children had yet seen. The ropes that suspended the platform were reinforced with enormous, thick chains. When the goblins saw the giant salamander, lying as if dead in the clearing, they all huddled together, as far from the great body as possible.

"It's okay," said Jack. "He's dead." Beside Eddie, out of sight of the goblins, the frog was whispering into the salamander's ear.

"HURRY UP!" came the imperious cry from above. The goblins reluctantly moved toward the salamander until they stood nine at a leg. Then they began hauling, dragging Eddie toward the platform.

Jack watched Eddie carefully. It looked like he was trying not to smile. The frog, unnoticed by the grunting, heaving goblins, hopped awkwardly alongside Eddie's head as it dragged along the ground. The goblins finally managed to get Eddie onto the platform.

"WE DID IT!" one of them shouted up to Begehren. From above came the sound of giant cranks turning, and then, very, very slowly, the platform began to rise into the air. Jack scooped up the frog, and he and Jill clambered onto the platform with Eddie.

"Hey!" shouted the goblins in the pit.

"WHAT?" Begehren called down. The platform continued, slowly, to rise.

"THEY'RE ON THE PLATFORM!" one of the goblins shouted.

The enormous load came to an unsteady halt, suspended just a few feet above the ground. "WHAT?" Jack called up. "WHAT'S WRONG?"

There was silence from above. Then Begehren called back, "COVER THE CHILDREN!"

Thirty-six goblins turned and drew daggers from their belts and pointed them at Jack and Jill. Jack let his spear clatter from his hand to the ground below. The children raised their hands in surrender.

A goblin grinned darkly and called up, "OKAY!"

And the platform began to rise again.

Up and up and up past the glowing walls, through the obscurity of the sinkhole, toward the red light of the Goblin Kingdom went the platform, the goblins, the children, Eddie and, hiding just beside Eddie's great head, the frog. He continued to croak quietly in Eddie's ear, reminding him to keep perfectly still. Jill could see that Eddie was definitely trying not to smile.

Finally, the platform cleared the edge of the sinkhole. The children blinked and shielded their eyes, for though the Goblin Kingdom was dim, it was far brighter than either the sinkhole or Eddie's cave. Thousands of goblins had filled the square surrounding them. Upon seeing Eddie, they began shouting and falling back. All, that is, save Begehren. He stared with wide eyes.

"Get that thing off of the platform!" he cried. Two dozen more strong goblins surged forward and grabbed at Eddie's limbs.

But Jill smiled and said, "He can do it himself."

Begehren looked at her like she was crazy, and for one moment, the entire Goblin Kingdom seemed to stand still. Then the frog croaked something, and Eddie lifted his head and roared. A giant arc of fire burned the air above their heads.

The goblins began screaming. High, shrill cries of terror. They screamed and cried and surged in a mass away from the horrible beast.

Except for Begehren. Begehren stared, unmoving.

Eddie closed his mouth, reloaded, so to speak, and recommenced in spraying fire all around him. Half a mile away buildings exploded and caught fire and people screamed.

When Eddie finally closed his mouth, everything for half a

ADAM GIDWITZ

mile around was charred kindling and burned cinders. And there was a pile of melted flesh, just a few feet from where Begehren had been standing.

Eddie turned his curious little eyes on Jack and Jill and the frog. He roared again.

"He wants to know what to do now," said the frog.

"Tell him to come down here," said Jill. So the frog croaked at the salamander, and Eddie lowered his enormous pink head to the ground. Jill threw her arms around his nose. Jack did, too. The frog, in Jack's pocket, croaked sad good-byes to their giant, lovely, smelly friend. Then Eddie lifted his head high into the air and roared the most deafening roar he had ever roared. The children covered their ears and stared as fire spumed all the way to the great roof of the Goblin Kingdom, hundreds of yards above them.

"He says 'Good-bye,'" said the frog.

Eddie gave a little jump with his huge body, and the whole Goblin Kingdom shook. Houses in the distance cracked and tumbled to the ground. Then he turned and leaped back down into the sinkhole, sliding down the walls with a horrible tearing sound.

"I think he likes it down there," said the frog. "It's like a big, warm well."

Jack turned to Jill. Her face, her skin, was blistered and

covered in salamander stomach acid. As was his. "You look lovely," he told her.

Jill grinned and curtsied. "Why, thank you. You, on the other hand, smell like a cesspool."

They laughed. Then the two children took hands and walked through the now-deserted Goblin Kingdom, searching for a way back to the light.

CHAPTER ELEVEN

The Others

Once upon a time, two young heroes stood in a forest, their shoulders heaving, inhaling the fresh, familiar scent of redwood and pine needles. They had triumphed. In every way, they had triumphed. They had climbed an enormous beanstalk, they had killed murderous giants, they had evaded an evil mermaid, they had outwitted a kingdom of goblins, they had made friends with an enormous, fire-breathing salamander, and they had won a mirror so rare and powerful a king could trade his kingdom for it and be counted a wise man. They had won the Seeing Glass.

At least, they were pretty sure it was the Seeing Glass. It was still so caked in Eddie's stomach juices that they weren't even certain it was a mirror, much less *the* mirror. But what else could it be? Meas, the giant guard, had told them the Glass was with the goblins. Begehren, the goblin leader, had told them Eddie had it. Eddie told them it was in his stomach, right next to his intestines. And this little disc was lodged right between Eddie's stomach and Eddie's intestines. So it was probably the Glass.

After leaving Eddie, Jack and Jill had made their way through the dark, nearly empty Goblin Kingdom. The goblins had all fled the return of the terrible Eidechse von Feuer, der Menschenfleischfressende, but they had also blockaded the ramps to the surface, to keep the beast under the earth. So the children had wandered and wended, scrounging for food and counting the days.

At last, they had found a tunnel in a black rock wall and had followed it up, and up, and up. It led, finally, into a sandstone cave, and the cave led out into this pine forest.

Excited, anxious, they moved out into the red-barked trees. Soon, they came to a road. It was red dirt and well worn and looked, strangely, familiar. Around the bend appeared a flock of sheep, and, herding them from behind, a young boy. As he passed, Jill called out, "Excuse me! Where does this road lead?"

The boy shouted back, over the bleating of his sheep, "To the kingdom, of course!"

"Which kingdom?" Jack asked.

ADAM GIDWITZ

The boy looked at Jack like he was stupid. "Märchen!"

Jack and Jill looked at each other, and then looked down the road, and then looked at each other again.

Here they were. Home again, home again, jiggedy jig.

Fear and excitement made their fingers tingle, their breath fast, their hearts beat crazily in their chests as Jack and Jill walked down the road toward the kingdom of Märchen.

What will my mother say? Jill wondered.

What will Marie and the boys say? Jack wondered.

What moronic things will the salamanders say? the frog tried his hardest not to wonder.

But as Jack's and Jill's minds wandered down those old lanes again, something tickled at the back of their thoughts. A new wisdom, still unformed and uncertain. A wisdom that had been creeping up on them throughout their terrible journey. A realization that, perhaps, they had been con-fused all along. Perhaps they had, all along, been looking for the wrong things.

This was a very wise thought indeed.

But beware, dear reader. For we go out into the wide, wild world, looking to change, looking to grow, looking for wisdom.

But wisdom is hard to come by, and once achieved, it is very easily lost. Especially when one is leaving the wide, wild world— and returning to the place you once fled.

More, though, than all of these questions and worries and prickings of new wisdom, Jack and Jill wondered whether the grimy disc that Jill carried really was the Seeing Glass. And what would happen—what would really happen—if it were not.

So preoccupied were the children that they barely noticed all the people that passed them on the road. They did not notice the fat man who was carrying his prize goat in his arms to see the doctor in town, nor the young woman with four baskets of fresh-picked wildflowers to sell at the castle.

They did not notice a man with a round face and pale blue eyes lugging two enormous cases of silks, who eyed them for a moment as he passed by. They did not notice an old woman with the face of a baby who hobbled along with a stick and watched them for just a moment too long. They did not even notice when a great cart rattling with bottles of potions and elixirs passed, and a man with long black hair and missing teeth peered out at the two children, smiled, and hurried his nag ahead.

Nor did they notice when the road forked and they, without

even thinking about it, followed the smaller, lonelier fork that led them under the heavy branches of dark trees. They did not notice when the path became narrower and narrower and narrower. They did not notice that the light was falling, the air was cold, the smell of the pines became sharp like winter.

But they absolutely *did* notice when the path ended altogether, and they found themselves in a clearing of towering trees, a ramshackle cart parked off to one side, and an enormous stone mansion tucked into the dark pine needles. Three people stood on the steps of the stone mansion, watching Jack and Jill expectantly: a round-faced silk merchant; a dirty, ponytailed snake-oil salesman; and a bent old woman with a baby's face. All three followed the children with eyes so pale they were almost white.

Jack and Jill stopped dead in their tracks.

"You return!" said the old woman. "How nice."

"Do you have the Glass?" asked the silk merchant, stepping down from the stone steps and walking toward them.

"They would be foolish indeed to return without it," added the ponytailed man, following close behind.

Jack opened his mouth. No sound came out. Jill looked from the old woman to the silk merchant and back again. She stammered, "You . . . you know each other?"

The three pale-eyed people grinned.

"Know each other? We're siblings!"

Jack closed his eyes tight and shook his head. He opened his eyes again.

"They call us the Others," said the silk merchant silkily. And something Begehren had said echoed in the children's memories.

"And we have been watching you," continued the old woman, "for a long, long time. We thought, perhaps, you were special. That you would, perhaps, be able to get the Glass. Were you?"

Jack turned to Jill. She took a deep breath, and then she held out the disc, encrusted with Eddie's stomach juices.

"What is that?" the ponytailed man demanded.

"Don't play with us, children," said the silk merchant, his pale eyes glowing in the dusk. "We had a bargain. You remember the terms."

The two men stepped closer to Jack and Jill. The shadow of the great house enveloped them all. Its windows twinkled with yellow candles.

The snake-oil salesman snarled. "Have you failed us? That is not the Glass."

The silk merchant grabbed it from Jill's hands. He turned it over. "What is this crud on it?"

Jill swallowed. Jack said, "From the stomach of the Eidechse von Feuer, die Menschenfleischefressende."

The Others stared at the children. Then the old woman reached for the disc and said, "Let me see that." The silk merchant gave it to her, and the Others huddled around. The dusky light, gray and blue and yellow, filtered through the trees. The old woman drew a deep breath, and then began to chant:

> *Mirror, mirror, of the truth,*
> *Old in years, long of tooth,*
> *Reveal to us your honest hue;*
> *Shine to us like you were new!*

Around the disc, the three strange figures bowed and hummed. Then they all began to make disgusting gurgling sounds in their throats. Finally, they all spat on the disc. The old woman rubbed it with her elbow.

Suddenly, in the clearing, there was a light much brighter than the dying light of dusk. It shone clear and clean and silver and true out of the small disc.

"Yes . . ." the old woman murmured. "I think it is . . . It may be . . ."

The silk merchant said, "We must test it! We must try it!"

The oil salesman was grinning like an idiot and clapping his hands together. "At last! At last!"

"Come with us," the old woman said to the children. "We will try it. And then you shall have your reward!"

Something about the way she said this did not inspire joy in Jack and Jill. They wondered why.

The foyer of the great stone house was grand and bright, with rich carpets on the floor and paintings in gilded frames hanging from the walls.

"You have a lovely home," Jill said politely.

"Thank you, my dear," replied the old woman. As she said it, the oil salesman bolted the front door behind them. Jack saw him pocket a large iron key. The old woman said, "We need some time with the Glass. To ensure that it is indeed what you say it is. Feel free to look around."

Jack and Jill watched the three pale-eyed Others disappear through a small door. It shut quietly. The children looked at one another.

"Let's get out of here!" the frog hissed, hidden deep in Jack's pocket.

Jill looked to Jack. "Maybe, for once, we should listen to him. I don't trust them."

ADAM GIDWITZ

"Too bad," said Jack. He gestured at the heavy door, bolted shut. "They have the key."

"We can try a window," said the frog.

"Come on," Jack gestured. "Let's just have a look around."

"I say we start by looking at the windows," the frog insisted.

They began to explore the house. Each room was different, and each more luxurious than the last. Great beds sat on plush rugs or shining, polished floors; the wallpaper was a riot of color in one room and a luscious cream in another; grand salons sat silently under towering, painted ceilings.

As they explored each room, the children's nervousness grew. What if it wasn't the Glass after all? What would the Others do? They wouldn't really *kill* them, right?

Furthermore, they noticed that the house had no windows.

"I don't get it," the frog murmured. "There were windows on the outside. Lots of them."

Jack wiped his brow with his sleeve and found that it was wet. Jill had begun chewing her bottom lip.

"What's taking them so long?" Jill wondered.

"Do you think that's a good sign, or a bad sign?" Jack asked.

"Bad sign," said the frog. "Definitely a bad sign."

They were on the first floor again. Jill walked to the front door and tried it. It would not budge.

"I'm going to ask," said Jack. His hand was on the door to the Others' room.

"I wouldn't," Jill said.

"Me neither," agreed the frog.

But Jack turned the knob and opened the door. He peered in. The room was empty.

"Where are they?" Jack asked, scratching his head.

"Did they leave when we were looking around?" Jill wondered.

"I do not like this," the frog said. "I do not like this at all."

The room was not quite as spacious or grand as the others, but it had a definite, delicate beauty. The floor was covered with a rug as deep and pure a blue as the sea. And, like the sea, it seemed to rock and shimmer beneath them. Around its border was a filigree of golden thread that looked for all the world like the pristine coast of a magical land. The children were mesmerized. "Look at this stuff . . ." muttered Jack. Against the wall stood a chest. Inside were stacked bar upon bar of gold that glittered red instead of yellow. Jill examined a small cherrywood box, sitting on a side table. Cautiously, she opened it. High ethereal music rose from within: *"Come, come, where heartache's never been . . ."* Jill shut it quickly and shivered. She looked at Jack. He hadn't heard a thing. He was examining the plush blue rug.

"Where are they?" Jill whispered.

"Not here. Let's go," said the frog.

Jack had lifted a corner of the rug. Its blue shifted, the golden border spreading out into the middle, as if the water of the sea were draining away. And then Jack said, "Here. They're here."

Jill moved to his side. Under the rug was a large, stone trapdoor.

"That's weird," said Jill quietly.

"Yes, it is," replied Jack.

"Why would they hide that?" Jill asked.

For a moment, no one uttered a word. And then Jack said, "Why don't we find out?"

And now, dear reader, I will give you a little warning. I have not warned you much through the course of this book (and occasionally I forgot to until it was too late—sorry about that).

But now I must indeed warn you. I do not know if little children are reading, or hearing, this book. After all that revolting bloodshed with the giants, and then the goblins, not to mention that horrible scene with the mermaid and the drowned girl, I certainly hope they are not.

THE OTHERS

But in case they are, or in case older children are reading this story and do not appreciate having the bejeezus scared out of them, or in case you are an adult and you just aren't really in the mood to be upset, I warn all of you:

This next part is not so nice.

It took both children, using all of their combined might, to lift the heavy stone trapdoor. Behind it, beneath it, was darkness. The small flames of the candles in the room fluttered as a rush of wind came up from the pit.

"Uh, guys?" said the frog, peering just above the edge of Jack's pocket. "We're not going down there, right?"

But Jack and Jill had come too far, done too much, to turn back now. Besides, the only door to the house was locked, and there were no windows. Where else could they go?

"Okay?" said Jill.

"Okay," said Jack.

"*Not* okay," said the frog.

Jill reached her foot probingly into the impenetrable gloom. Her foot touched something. She put weight on it. The something held.

She stood on the something and reached her foot forward

again. Again, she found something to rest on. She shifted her weight carefully. This something, too, held her. And now she could tell what the somethings were. They were stairs.

Jack and Jill, holding hands, descended into the heart of the darkness.

One step, and the children stopped. One more step, and they stopped again. The stairs were not even, but rather knobby and irregular. They twisted around and around in a tight spiral. Jack's and Jill's clasped hands were slick, and they held onto one another so hard they could not feel their own fingers. One more step. And another. And another.

And then the obscurity was softened—there rose, from beneath, an eerie, flickering yellow. A few more steps, and Jack and Jill found a candle that seemed to hang, suspended, in the darkness. Jack reached out his hand and found a curving wall. It was not smooth. It was strangely ridged, oddly bumpy. He let his hand trail along it as they descended to the floating candle.

When they were but a few steps away from it, they began to make out what held the candle up. It was a strange candlestick, extended from the wall. The candlestick was long and straight and smooth in the middle, but at either end was a rounded protrusion. Even in the flickering yellow candlelight, the children could see that the candlestick was white. Bone white.

And then Jill was screaming. Jack turned around, threw his arms around her, and then, because she would not stop screaming, he clapped his hand over her mouth. Jill's eyes were wide, and they were rolling around in her head. Jack whispered, "What? What?" But still her eyes rolled. He tried to follow their frantic gaze. He looked at the candlestick. Then he followed the wall down. Then he examined the stairs that they were standing on. A cry rose to Jack's lips, but he clamped them shut and held it in. The candlestick, the walls, the stairs were made of human bones.

"Run!" the frog cried. "Run!" Jack's hand shot out and clamped his mouth shut, too.

Jack's and Jill's eyes locked in the darkness.

They stood up.

Okay.

Imagine you were over at someone's house. Let's say for a playdate.

Your friend disappears for a moment, and you happened to go looking for her. You look all over the place. Then you look in the basement.

And let's say that you discover that the basement was composed entirely of human bones.

ADAM GIDWITZ

I hope, in such a situation, that you would do the sensible thing—and run away as fast as you possibly could.

In other words, I hope that you would not do what Jack and Jill did.

For Jack and Jill had seen cruel giants, and murderous mermaids, and child-snatching goblins, and Eddie. It was going to take more than a bone staircase to make them run now. Once on their feet, they pushed the horror in their chests down as far as they could, clasped hands once more, and started down the stairs again.

The staircase twisted around and around, and now distantly spaced candles in candlesticks of bone lit their way, leaving just a single stair in complete obscurity before the dim light of the next candle made their horrible surroundings visible again.

And then the stairs ended, and a series of candles lit a long hall. Jill covered her mouth. Jack looked away. The walls, the ceiling, the floor were all made of bone.

Down the long, gruesome corridor, Jack and Jill saw a square where the flickering candlelight was brighter. Slowly, walking as silently as they knew how, they approached it. It was a doorway.

Stronger candlelight danced through it. Jack looked at Jill. She nodded.

Slowly—so slowly that you would not have seen him moving if you did not know that he was—Jack extended the edge of his head past the bone door frame, until nothing more than his ear and his eye would have been visible within the room.

Jack jerked his head back.

Jill stared at him. He gestured for her to do as he had done. Just as slowly, just as imperceptibly, Jill moved her head so that with a single eye she could see the contents of the room.

The first thing she saw was a light fixture—an enormous chandelier, in fact—hanging from the center of the chamber. It was suspended from the vaulted ceiling by tangled cords of rib bones, interlocking crazily. Below them hung the nine-pointed chandelier, each point made of a skull resting on a platter of pelvises. Strung between the nine points were femurs, hanging like laundry from a drooping line. The chandelier was covered with candles, dripping their yellow tallow over the white bones. Jill's gaze ran upward to the ceiling. It gave new meaning to the term rib vaulting. Ribs were extended in undulating curves from the top of the walls to the center of the ceiling, where a line of skulls smiled down at Jill. And one could tell, from the chandelier, from the ceiling, from the walls and the floor, that these were not just any human bones. They were the bones of children.

From the rib vaulted ceiling, long cords of rope hung taut,

and at the end of each cord was a sack. A yellowed, bloodstained sack. Just about the size of a child's body.

Below these sacks, in the center of the room, stood a bone altar. On it sat a shining circle. It was, without any doubt, the Seeing Glass, its surface now perfectly clean, perfectly clear.

Before the Glass, before the shrine of bone, knelt the three Others.

"Please!" the silk merchant moaned. "Show us your secrets, great Glass! Give us your wisdom!"

The Seeing Glass sat on the altar, silent.

"What must we do for you?" pleaded the oil merchant. "Mirror of truth! Show us your power! We beg you!"

The Seeing Glass stared down from its shrine, impassive.

"Guiding light of the Goblin Kingdom . . ." intoned the old woman. "Repository of the world's greatest secrets . . . Giver of power . . . Keeper of truth . . . Please . . ."

"We are so close . . ." the silk merchant whispered.

"We have sought ye a thousand years . . ." murmured the oil salesmen.

"Please!" cried the old woman. "PLEASE!"

Nothing.

The old woman sighed bitterly—a sigh of a thousand years of frustration—and lifted herself to her feet. "I will try to read the spell again," she said. She approached the Glass. Jack's and Jill's heads now both peered, ever so carefully, around the bone door frame.

The old woman bent her silvery head over the glass. *"Fo timb hat da jeek, bok no father,"* she read. *"Fo timb hat da jeek, bok no father! Fo timb hat da jeek, bok no father!"*

"What the heck does that mean?" whispered the frog. Jack clamped his mouth shut again.

"EVERYONE!" she bellowed. "EVERYONE CHANT IT!"

"Fo timb hat da jeek, bok no father!" they chanted. *"Fo timb hat da jeek, bok no father! Fo timb hat da jeek, bok no father!"*

"It isn't working!" the old woman cried. "It doesn't work!"

"They will pay!" the silk merchant bellowed, on his feet now. "Just like all of the other children have paid for failing!" And he gestured violently at the bones and bloody sacks above their heads.

Jack's and Jill's eyes followed his gesture and then met. Jill jerked her head toward the stairs. Jack nodded and straightened up.

"Yes . . ." muttered the old woman. "We must admit it. They have failed." She shook her head.

"I bet they'll taste good, though," the oil salesman shrugged. "That is a small consolation."

The children's faces went white.

ADAM GIDWITZ

Jill made a small movement toward the stairs.

Jack, on the other hand, stepped into the room.

Jill turned, saw Jack, and had a heart attack. The frog had two. In a row.

The Others spun. For a moment, they stared, too stunned to speak.

And then the old woman managed to say, "Just who we were looking for."

The two men moved toward Jack and clamped their hands around his thin arms. "Hello there," said the silk merchant.

"It turns out," smiled the oil merchant, "that this Glass of yours isn't all it's cracked up to be." Their grips felt like they would crush Jack's bones.

"Turns out," the silk merchant agreed, "it's a fake."

The old woman shook her head. "And we *did* have a deal."

Jack's chin was set and his eyes were flashing like flint when he said, "Let us try. Let us try to make it work." Jill was standing in the doorway behind him, watching him, trembling.

The old woman slid up to Jack and lifted her face to his. "You have an hour to make the Glass work. Our patience has expired."

And she swept past him, past Jill, and out of the chamber of bone. The silk merchant flashed Jack a smile. For the first time,

Jack noticed that his teeth were like pins, tiny and sharp, sticking up from blue gums. Jack shuddered. The silk merchant laughed and left. The oil salesman followed him.

Jack and Jill walked up to the Seeing Glass, now clean and clear. They brought their faces before its shining pane.

In the Glass, Jack saw a boy. His face was lined with sweat and caked with filth. His mouth was set in fear.

In the Glass, Jill saw a girl. Her hair was wet and matted to her forehead. Her skin was blistering and deathly pale.

Above their faces, along the top of the Glass, ran a strange script. It read, *"Fo timb hat da jeek, bok no father."*

"What does it mean?" whispered the frog, peering from Jack's pocket.

Jack and Jill shook their heads.

"This is it?" asked Jill. "It just looks like a mirror."

Jack picked it up from the bone altar. *"Fo timb hat da jeek, bok no father,"* he muttered. Then he shrugged. "How do you think it works?"

Jill rubbed the silvered pane. Nothing happened.

Jack shook the Glass. Nothing.

The frog begged it: "Please do something! Please! Please?" Of course, nothing.

"I don't understand," said Jack. "Begehren said it was the greatest treasure in the world."

"Even Meas said it was worth looking for," Jill agreed.

So they redoubled their efforts. They tried everything they could think of to make it work, from singing to it to wearing it like a hat. Nothing helped.

The hour was nearly gone.

"I give up!" Jill cried at last. "Forget it! It's just a stupid mirror!"

"*Now* she says it's a stupid mirror," says the frog. "*Now* that we've gone to the sky, and underground, and are trapped in a room of bone by psychopathic cannibals. *Now* it's just a stupid mirror."

Jack muttered, "They'll kill us. They'll kill us."

The children sat down. Above their heads, the body bags swung slowly at the end of creaking twine. A few drops of blood fell to the bone floor between the two children.

"Oh God . . ." Jill groaned.

"Okay, that's it, good-bye," said the frog. "I'm going to go hide. They've never seen me, as far as I know. As far as I know, they don't know I exist. So I'm just going to hide. Sorry, guys. Good luck to you. Good-bye." He hopped from Jack's shirt and began looking for a place to stow himself until the carnage was over. "I'd stay and die with you," he added, "but this was *not* my idea. In fact, as you recall, I counseled you against this course of action about, I don't know, a *thousand times.*"

"They've never seen you . . ." Jack murmured.

Jill let her head collapse in her hands.

"They've never seen you," Jack repeated, standing up.

"So?" said Jill.

"So I'm going to survive this thing yet!" announced the frog.

"They've never seen you!" Jack grinned.

Jill and the frog looked at Jack like he was crazy.

Ten minutes later, the Others slid back into the room. Their faces were dark, but their eyes were bright.

"Well?" said the silk merchant. "Have you prepared yourselves?"

"With salt and rosemary, perhaps?" the oil salesman smiled.

Jack and Jill spun from the mirror at the same time.

"It works!" they both cried excitedly. "It works!" Jill ran to the old woman and grabbed her arm. "Come see!" she cried. "Come see!" Jack was standing by the mirror, grinning madly.

The three Others rushed to the Glass. They peered into it. "What?" demanded the old woman. "How? I can't see anything!" She was shaking, as if the anticipation of this moment was too much for her. "Show me!" she barked. "Show me!"

Jill said, "Step back."

All three Others stepped back at once, their eyes glued to the Glass.

And Jill said,

> Mirror, mirror, on the wall,
> Who is the fairest of them all?

And, from deep within the altar of bone, a voice resounded:

> In eye, in cheek, in hair, in hand,
> The queen is the fairest in the land.

"IT WORKS!" the Others screamed. "IT WORKS!" Their cries rumbled from the pits of their bellies and ended in a screech so high it hurt Jack's and Jill's ears. "IT WORKS!"

The old woman grabbed Jill. "Do it again! Ask it another question!"

Jill took a deep breath.

> Mirror, mirror, tell me, sing,
> Of the giants, who is king?

And the mirror replied,

Great of arm but weak of head,
Aitheantas was. Now he's dead.

"IT KNOWS!" the old woman shrieked. "IT KNOWS EVERYTHING!"

"How does it work?" the silk merchant demanded, grabbing Jack by the arm. "How did you get it to work?"

"The same way you cleaned it," Jack explained. "Call it 'Mirror, Mirror.' Then rhyme your question."

"That's it?" exclaimed the oil salesman. "That's all there is to it?"

Jack shrugged. "That's all."

"Out of the way!" the oil salesman bellowed. He pushed Jack and Jill aside. He took a deep breath.

Mirror, mirror, on the wall,
Make me the king of Märchen!

Jack looked at Jill. She tried to suppress a smile. "Uh," Jack said, "that didn't rhyme."

"What?" the oil salesman demanded. "It didn't?"

"No," said Jill. "And it wasn't a question. The Glass only seems to answer questions."

The silk merchant pushed his brother out of the way and approached the Glass. He said,

> *Mirror, mirror, king of men,*
> *When will my life come to an end?*

The mirror was silent. A drop of sweat slid down the side of Jack's face.

But finally, the mirror spoke:

> *Obey this Glass, through good and ill,*
> *And die? Oh no, you never will.*

"I KNEW IT!" shrieked the silk merchant, leaping into the air with a scream of demented joy.

The old woman howled: "LIVE FOREVER! We'll LIVE FOREVER! *We've done it! We've done it!*"

The Others began to dance around the bone chamber, spinning and leaping and hugging themselves. The silk merchant banged the bones of the wall with his fists and shouted. The oil salesman slapped himself in the face over and over again.

Finally, the obscene celebrations stopped, and the old woman approached the altar. She wiped the sweat of joy from her brow and intoned,

Mirror, mirror, on the wall,
Who is the cleverest of them all?

The mirror paused. And then it replied,

Up a stalk or down a hill,
None is as clever as Jack and Jill.

The Others were about to begin leaping and whooping in celebration again when they caught themselves.

"What?" demanded the old woman. "What did it say?"

Jack and Jill looked at each other, apparently befuddled. "It said we were," Jill shrugged.

"That's not possible!" barked the silk merchant. "*We* have the Glass! *We*, who have been seeking it for a thousand years! *We* have it!"

"You're asking the wrong question!" the oil salesman exclaimed. "Here, let me try."

Mirror, mirror, on the wall,
Who is the bravest of them all?

This time the Glass did not hesitate.

Up a stalk or down a hill,
None is as brave as Jack and Jill.

"NO!" screamed the Others, all together. "NO! It isn't possible! How could it be?"

"*We* are the cleverest!"

"*We* are the bravest!"

"Aren't we?"

"Aren't we?"

"Aren't we?" they all howled.

The oil salesman came right up to the Seeing Glass and peered into its crystalline face. "Please, Glass, please. We are the bravest, aren't we? Aren't we, Glass? Aren't we? Tell us we are!"

"Let me ask!" the silk merchant demanded. Everyone moved back, and he chanted:

Mirror, mirror, on the wall,
Who is the wisest of them all?

And the voice of the Glass rang out like a brazen trumpet:

———

Up a stalk or down a hill,

None is as wise as Jack and Jill!

The chamber resounded with a scream so heart-wrenching and terrible that it would have brought you to your knees. *"No!"* the Others howled. "Tell us it isn't so! Say it is not so!"

But it was so. The Glass had decreed it.

"How is it possible?" the Others screamed. "They are children! Stupid children!"

"They are not clever!"

"They are not brave!"

"They aren't even smart!"

"Not wise like us! None is as wise as us!"

And then Jack said, "You can ask *why* it thinks we're so brave and wise and clever."

"Or," suggested Jill, "maybe it can tell you how to be even better than us?"

The old woman looked at her, eyes burning and demented. "Yes!" she cried. "Yes, of course! Now that we have the Glass, we can know exactly what to do! Move aside!"

So everyone moved aside, and she bellowed,

Mirror, mirror, tell us true,

To be the greatest, what should we do?

There was a long silence. In the bone chamber, the only sound was the dripping of blood from the body bags overhead and the Others' frantic, ragged breathing.

Finally, the mirror answered:

Jack and Jill braved terrors en masse

To find, and recover, this sacred Glass.

Ye three have lived a life of sin.

To prove your worth, turn yourselves in.

Go to the guards of the royal throne.

Show them your victims. Show them their bones.

If you can face justice without fear,

Then soon, your own names from this Glass you'll hear.

The Glass fell silent again. The Others stared at it, frozen.

"Turn ourselves in?" the oil salesman muttered.

Jack and Jill watched the Others' faces tensely.

"Face justice?" said the silk merchant. "But surely, they'll put us to death."

But the old woman raised her voice.

> *Mirror, mirror, master of fate,*
> *If we do this, will we be great?*

And the mirror answered,

> *Face the punishment, standing tall,*
> *And ye shall indeed be the greatest of all.*

"We will be!" the old woman crowed. "*We will be!*" And then she barked at her two siblings, "Come on!"

She ran from the room. For a moment, the two men continued to gaze at the Glass. Then, slowly, resolutely, they turned and followed their sister.

For nearly twenty minutes, neither Jack nor Jill said a word. They merely stood, stock-still, listening to the pounding of their hearts, praying that indeed the Others were gone.

Finally, the Glass intoned, "Well, that must have been the *greatest* performance in the history of Märchen." The frog crawled out of a hole between two rib bones at the base of the altar. He was beaming.

"It was pretty good," Jack grinned.

"*Pretty good?* It was *great*! It was *genius*! I am a dramatic *genius*!"

Jack laughed. "You may indeed be a dramatic genius."

"I am indeed," the frog agreed. But then he paused. "Still, I can't believe they fell for it! Why did they fall for it?"

Jill replied, "Didn't you see how they worshipped the Glass, even before it spoke? Didn't you recognize that from somewhere?"

Jack said, "I know I did."

"They are con-fused," said Jill.

"With the Glass," said Jack.

The children stared at the Seeing Glass.

"Maybe," said the frog. "Or maybe I am just a dramatic genius."

CHAPTER TWELVE

Face to Face

Once upon a time, two children walked down a long, dusty road.

Jack fingered the Glass from time to time. He shook his head at it. Its secrets remained locked away.

Jill wondered about the Others. She wondered where they were, and if they were following the mirror's advice. She watched the road warily.

The children's stomachs were all tied up in knots, and their throats had lumps that made it hard to breathe. But not just because of the Others. Nor solely because of the Glass.

Their stomachs were in knots and their throats were thick with lumps because, at long last, they were returning to the places they had fled, the people they had run from. They were, at long last, going home.

They came to a fork in the road.

"I go this way," said Jack.

Jill nodded. "I go this way."

They embraced.

"Oh," said Jack. "Do you want the Glass? I don't know what to do with it."

Jill shook her head. "You keep it. We don't need another mirror in my house."

Jack grinned sideways. "Sure," he said. And then he whispered, "Good luck."

"Good luck," Jill whispered back.

Then they parted.

As Jack made his way over the small country roads that led to his father's house, he saw a group of boys playing blindman's bluff in a field. Marie was the blind man. His eyes were closed, and he stumbled around after the other boys as they dipped and dodged out of his way.

"Hi," said Jack. Some of the boys turned to him.

"Who's that?" Marie called, his eyes still tightly shut.

"It's me," said Jack. "Jack."

Marie's eyes flew open. All the boys were staring now.

Marie asked, "What happened to you?"

Jack grinned. "A lot. Remember when I bought that bean? Well, then—"

"No," said Marie. "I mean, what happened to your skin? Did you fall in a toilet or something?" The boys exploded with laughter.

Jack looked down at his skin. It did look disgusting. He said, "I got this from going in the stomach of a fire-breathing beast!"

"That's funny. My toilet breathes water," said Marie, and the boys roared.

"I did!" Jack insisted. "I did!"

The boys laughed harder.

Jack stood, staring at them. A dim and distant wisdom tickled his brain. He shook it off and turned for his house. He came to the front door. He took a deep breath.

Before he could take the doorknob, the door opened itself. His father stood in the doorway.

A moment of silence.

And then, "Jack?"

Jack nodded.

Jack's father threw his arms around his son.

———

Jack's father made him some food, he helped him wash himself, and he told Jack to lie down. He needn't worry about chores for a little while. He looked like he'd had a rough time of it.

"I missed you," his father said. "I feel bad about how I acted."

Jack nodded. But he was already staring out the window, watching the boys play blindman's bluff.

The next day, he was outside with them, going with them down to the river, running with them across the fields.

Soon, that old song came back.

Marie had a little lamb, little lamb, little lamb. Marie had a little lamb whose fleece was black as coal.

"Don't sing that," Jack would say. "It isn't funny." So the boys would sing it louder.

Everywhere that Marie went, Marie went, Marie went, everywhere that Marie went the lamb was sure to go.

"Please stop!"

It made the children laugh and play, laugh and play, laugh and play, it made the children laugh and play to see the lamb follow.

"STOP IT!" Jack would shout. And the boys would roar with laughter.

Jack tried to just be with the boys. Not follow them. Just be with them. He even tried to tell them of the places he'd been, the things he'd done. But they didn't believe him. Jack was a dreamer. And a follower. Always was, always would be.

286   ADAM GIDWITZ

They teased him mercilessly. And when they weren't teasing him, they were mocking each other. Jack hated it.

And the song. The song would not go away.

Marie had a little lamb, little lamb . . .

And then, one day, Jack had had enough.

Marie had been teasing him for hours, calling him "toilet" for his blisters and scabbing skin, and asking why he followed them around so much. The boys sang the lamb song again and again and again.

Jack stood there, taking it, trying to laugh—as his face turned red and he squinted his eyes against the tears.

Just then, out of the corner of his eye, he saw three ravens fly past. He did not know if they were the talking ravens or not. They could have been regular ravens, for all he knew.

But when he saw them, he remembered something that the talking ravens had said. Something he had not understood at the time. *When you do what you want, not what you wish . . .*

And suddenly he realized, *I wish I could be friends with these boys. But I do not want to be. I do not think I like them at all.*

And without another word, he turned around and walked away.

It was one week earlier that Jill left the frog on the edge of the well and promised she'd come and visit him soon.

He looked unhappily into the mossy, smelly darkness. "You'd better . . ." he said. She smiled.

Jill headed for the front of the castle. She started walking very slowly, her stomach turning over and over. Then she walked faster. And faster. And faster. Soon, she was running. She came to the castle gate.

The guards took one look at her and said, "Princess?" Jill nodded, her eyes brimming, her throat too thick for words.

"The princess is home!" they shouted. "The princess is home!" The call was taken up all throughout the castle. Jill ran to the great door, and then through the grand hall, and finally up the steps that led to the throne room. And as she ran, she heard, "The princess is home! The princess is home!" echoing from the walls, and also laughter, and whooping, and even some weeping.

Jill burst into the throne room. Her father jumped nearly a foot at the sound of the door banging open. He cried, "Darling!" But Jill ran for her mother. Her mother had turned, and her eyes were wide like moons, and Jill catapulted herself into her arms. And, burying her face in her mother's neck, she said, "Mommy."

And her mother held her. But not tightly.

At last, Jill pulled back.

Her mother looked slightly disgusted. "Darling . . ." she began. "What's happened to you . . . ?"

"Well," said Jill, "it's a long story. It starts with a beanstalk. No, it starts with a frog, who can—"

But her mother cut her off. "No," said her mother. "I mean, what's happened to your skin, darling?"

Jill felt like she had been punched in the gut. She took a step back. She looked at the floor. She said, "Sorry, Mommy. I'll go wash."

So Jill got washed up as best she could, put ointment on her blisters, put on all the correct clothes, and went back to her life as it had been before—sitting by her mother's side as the queen reapplied makeup or fussed with her hair.

But it didn't feel right.

From time to time, she would tell her mother how beautiful she looked. And her mother would blush and deny it and smile, just as she always had.

But now, this ritual reminded Jill of goblins and a throne and silken bonds.

One day, her mother was testing new shades of eye shadow, and Jill was bored. She stared out the window, remembering that fateful day with the beggar. Then, suddenly, across the square, she espied three dark forms. Her heart caught.

Birds, she realized. They were black birds, casting long shadows on a windowsill. Perhaps ravens. She smiled to think that, maybe, they knew the future . . .

Suddenly, Jill was reminded of something the ravens had said to her. *When you no longer seek your reflection in others' eyes* . . .

She thought of the Others' pale eyes. Then she thought of her mother.

At that very instant, the queen looked up at her. "Darling, will you go put some more makeup on? Your blisters are starting to show again."

Jill felt the familiar twisting in her stomach that she was again growing used to living at home. But she swallowed it down. She took a deep breath. She tried a new approach. "It's just the two of us here, Mommy. And I don't really care about my skin."

"Well, I do! It looks dreadful! You look dreadful!" And the queen went back to testing eye shadow.

Jill stared at her beautiful mother. And then, very slowly, she reached for a heavy silver hairbrush that sat on a side table.

The queen was too busy admiring a new shade of blue to notice. Nor did she notice Jill pull the brush back behind her head. But she certainly did notice the brush crash into the large silver mirror and send it shivering, shattering, into a million pieces.

"I DON'T CARE!" Jill screamed.

Jill's mother turned around, mouth agape, eyes as wide as moons.

An anger and a hurt so deep, so old, exploded from the little girl. "I DON'T CARE WHAT YOU THINK! I DON'T CARE! You stare in that mirror all day long and you don't even see! *You don't even see!*"

And then Jill spun and ran.

The queen was frozen. At last, she shook herself, stood, and hurried to her chamber door. She looked down the hall. Empty. She looked back in her room. Her mirror was shattered.

And yet, in that moment, the queen was not concerned with the mirror. Not at all. She was much more concerned about something else. Someone else. Which she found very, very surprising.

"Jill!" she cried out. "JILL!"

But it was too late. Jill was gone.

Jill arrived at the well.

She stopped.

Jack was already sitting on the ledge. The light on his face was dappled by the bare trees. Birdsong echoed throughout the grove, as did the creaking of branches in the wind.

Jill sat down beside him. Neither said a word. They did not

have to. Jack pressed his lips together in a weak excuse for a smile. Jill put her arm around his shoulders.

Just then, the frog clambered up onto the edge of the well.

"Hooray! You're back!" he cried. "How'd it go? Good? Better than here, I hope. I thought Eddie was smelly. Jeez! A frog leaves his well for a year, comes home, and it's like they've been growing mold on purpose! In fact, they probably have! And stuuuupid! 'Hey Frog, where were you? Where was I? Where am I? Who am I? What is the meaning of life?' Idiots." The frog smiled up at the two children appealingly. Then his face fell. "What?" he said. "What's wrong?" He waited. "What, it didn't go too good?"

Jack and Jill shook their heads. "Not too good at all," said Jack.

The frog sighed. "No, 'You're so beautiful,' 'You're so great'?"

"No," said Jack.

"No," said Jill.

The birds sang in the trees as if nothing at all was wrong. The frog looked up. The sky was that deep, cerulean blue that he had once loved so.

"No, 'Home Sweet Home'?" the frog tried again.

"This isn't my home," said Jill.

Jack looked over at her.

She said, "Home is where you can be yourself."

ADAM GIDWITZ

Jack pressed his lips together. He nodded. He took her hand, picked up the frog, and stood up. Jill stood up, too.

And then Jack and Jill walked away.

As Jack and Jill walked, no destination in mind, they came to a very tall hill, just on the outskirts of town. Around the base of the hill, a large crowd had gathered. The two children came up and tried to ask what was going on, but no one would listen to them. All strained their necks to see the top of the hill.

Finally, Jack nudged a boy about his own age. "What is everybody looking at?" he asked.

The boy said, "Three murderers are being punished. They're to be rolled down this here hill." He was a small boy, with a sooty face and no front teeth.

"Rolled down a hill?" said Jack. "What kind of punishment is that?"

The boy grinned at Jack with his gap-toothed smile. "Well, they came to the royal guards and confessed to being murderers— and cannibals! So they were brought before a judge. Not just any judge. The Beggar Judge."

Jack and Jill shrugged.

"You don't know the Beggar Judge?" the boy exclaimed. "But he's famous! He's the beggar that gave his blanket to the princess when she was naked!" Jill blushed hotly and stared all the more intently at the boy, who went on, oblivious. "The king saw him do it, and, for being so kind and merciful, he made him a judge. And he's the best judge we've got. Wise and fair."

The boy continued, "Anyhow, the murderers were brought before the Beggar Judge. He asked them why they confessed. And you know what they said? They said, once they confessed, they would be the greatest, bravest, wisest creatures in the whole world! *Creatures.* That's what they said!" The boy was clearly enjoying the story. "So the judge said, 'If you're so wise, you can be my assistants, and help me be a judge!' Well, the murderers like that, don't they?" The boy took a deep breath, readying himself for the story's climax.

"Well, the first case they had to decide was that of a murderer. And the judge, he asked them what the punishment should be. And they said, put him in a barrel, drive nails into it, and roll him down a hill. They were pretty proud of themselves for that bit of wisdom. So the Beggar Judge, he says, 'You have pronounced your own sentence.' Just like that."

As the boy finished his tale, a terrible scream rose from the top of the hill, and three barrels started tumbling down the steep slope.

The barrels bounced and bounded over rocks and gullies, and with each bounce the screams grew more bloodcurdling

ADAM GIDWITZ

and horrible. And then, about two-thirds of the way down the hill, the screaming stopped altogether, and the barrels tumbled onward in eerie silence.

When they finally came to rest at the bottom of the hill, the crowd surged forward to pry open the barrels and inspect the bodies inside.

But Jack and Jill turned away. "They must have been very con-fused indeed," muttered Jill. Jack nodded.

And they left.

Jack and Jill had a new home. It was a small clearing, behind a tiny village on the outskirts of the kingdom of Märchen. They had no roof over their heads, nor even a natural canopy, for it was the dying days of winter, and no tree had leaves. When it rained, the children were soaked to the bone, and they huddled together and shivered. Rain at night was the worst. As they held each other against the freezing needles, the frog would sigh and say, "Even my well is better than this." But he stayed with them anyway.

During the day, Jack and Jill collected fallen sticks in the forest and laid them out in the center of their clearing to dry. Then they would bundle them up and take them into the village, going door-to-door, selling them as kindling, hoping for a penny for the whole bunch.

Most people refused them. "Ugh!" they would cry upon seeing the children on their doorstep. "It's those filthy orphans!" And they would slam the door in their faces.

Which was understandable. Jack and Jill did look pretty disgusting. They had not washed themselves for weeks now, and their skin was scabbing from the blisters, and their hair was matted, and their clothes stank.

Occasionally, someone would buy a fardel of twigs for their fireplace and pay the children a penny, and then Jack and Jill would trade that penny for a loaf of bread or a small round of cheese, and they would take their food back to the clearing and eat it hungrily. But most days, the children would just sit in the driving rain, huddled together on the muddy ground, the bare branches lashing against one another, wailing in the wind. Jack's arms would be around Jill, or hers around him, and the frog would curl up between them, and they would be pummeled by the rain or the sleet or the hail. And there was nothing at all they could do about it.

From time to time, they would take out the Seeing Glass. They would stare at it and think of all the mistakes that had brought them to this place. Foremost of which was going out to look for this stupid, useless mirror.

And then, as the days became weeks, and the weeks became months, things started to change.

The weather turned from late winter to early spring. Little buds appeared on the branches above where the children slept at night, and then the buds burst into white blossoms.

After collecting twigs for the day and laying them out in the sun to dry, Jack and Jill would play. Jack, you will remember, had the most incredible imagination. He would create fantastical scenarios and narrate them to Jill, and they would act them out—meeting dragons and speaking invented languages and finding buried treasures. Jill was the funny one. She would make these jokes that were so dry, Jack wouldn't recognize them as jokes, until the frog started laughing, and then Jack would start laughing, too, and keep laughing until his sides hurt.

The people of the village still shouted at them, and children would see them playing and tease them, even throw stones at them.

But the strangest thing was happening. Jack and Jill began not to care. They would run deeper into the woods, pretending they had been chased by giant, man-eating unicorns, or something equally ridiculous. Later, they would climb trees and leap from their branches. They would run headlong into a swollen, muddy stream and make balls of mud and hurl them at one another, and the frog would scream and they would keel over laughing. And then at night, they would lie under the stars, and the night was not as cold as it had once been, and Jack would think, *I had fun today.* And Jill would think, *I was happy with what I did.*

It was a strange sensation.

Do you know what is happening to Jack and Jill right now?

I'm not sure. But I think it is something like this:

There is this weird thing that happens, when you stop worrying so much about what other people think of you. When you are no longer—to use the ravens' word—con-fused.

At that moment, you suddenly start seeing what *you* think of you.

For the first time in their short lives, Jack and Jill felt free enough to see what they thought of themselves. And they were shocked to discover something very surprising indeed.

They were shocked to discover that they actually *liked themselves.*

They were funny and silly and imaginative, and very, very loving.

They'd never realized it before. But actually, they liked themselves quite a lot.

———

ADAM GIDWITZ

And then something even stranger happened. It was on a warm spring day. Jack and Jill were wading in the stream, lobbing mud balls at each other and laughing at the top of their lungs, when a small girl appeared in the trees at the edge of the stream.

Jill saw her and decided to ignore her. The girl was probably waiting to throw a rock at them.

But Jack saw her and stopped. When he did, one of Jill's lobbed mud balls hit him directly in the head. He stumbled. He looked up. The little girl, who had stringy orange hair that hung to her shoulders, put her hand up in front of her mouth. She was hiding a smile. Jack wiped the mud from his face and smiled back.

Jill hit him in the head with another ball of mud.

"Hey!" he shouted at her. Jill cackled. Jack turned back to the girl. "Do you want something?"

She continued to stare at them, shrugged, and then she said, "Can I play with you?"

Jack's mouth fell open. So did Jill's.

"Um . . ." said Jack. And then he said, "Uh . . . sure."

The little girl waded directly into the stream, leaned down and buried her hands in the muddy riverbed, collected a large ball of mud, and pelted Jack in the face with it.

"Hey!" he cried again. Jill squealed and threw another at

him. He bellowed, "Retreat! Retreat!" And the two girls went chasing him through the river, hurling mud balls after him.

The next day, the little girl—whose name was Elsie—was at the stream again. She had brought her little sister, who had the same orange hair and spatter of freckles. Jack and Jill were in a tree this time, inventing stories for each other.

"Can I come up?" Elsie asked. Jack gestured for her to join them.

"Can I?" echoed her little sister in a thin voice.

"Sure," said Jill. And she slid over on the branch to make room for the girls.

Over the course of the next week, a small group of children formed in the forest. Each day, in the warmth of the late afternoon, they would gather and play with Jack and Jill. And no one said anything about their skin or their clothes or where they lived. They just did not seem to care.

Soon, it was a regular ritual. Every day, after Jack and Jill had sold the last of their sticks, they would be greeted by a small group of boys and girls at their clearing in the wood. It felt good. It felt like home.

From time to time, Jack and Jill still took out the Glass. They peered into it, marveling at its perplexing uselessness.

"How did the goblins find it so valuable?" Jack wondered.

"Dunno," Jill shrugged. They studied it for a while longer. "Guess the whole quest was a waste," she concluded, tossing it aside.

"Yeah," Jack agreed.

But neither child felt that way. Not anymore. Not at all.

And then, one day, the frog poked his head out of the hollow log in the clearing. "Hey, guys! I figured something out!"

Jack lifted him out of the log.

"Get the Glass, too," the frog instructed Jill.

She looked at him oddly, and then reached down and withdrew the Glass from its hiding place in the log.

"Hold it up," the frog directed Jill. She held the Glass in front of him.

"Still looks like a fat old frog," said Jack.

The frog ignored him. "I think I know what it says."

Jack looked at the frog's reflection. "You know what *what* says?"

"The inscription, dummy!" cried the frog.

Suddenly, the children's expressions grew serious. Jill said, "It says, 'Fo timb hat da jeek, bok no father.'"

"Great wisdom," added Jack.

"Maybe it's in goblin . . ." Jill wondered.

"No, stop, listen for a second," the frog insisted. "It's not, 'Fo timb hat da jeek, bok no father.' That first letter isn't an *f*, it's a *t*."

"To?" Jill said slowly.

"And in the next word, it's not a *t*, it's an *f*."

Jack and Jill leaned more closely over the Glass.

"And an *n*, not an *m*, and, I guess, a weird looking *d*."

"How much time have you been spending on this?" Jack asked.

"A lot," said the frog. "And that's a *w*, not a decorative squiggle."

Jack leaned over, his finger on his lips, peering at the letters. "Oh . . ." he murmured.

"And that's a *y*, not a *d*. And an *e*, not an *a*."

"Where did you learn to read?" Jill asked suddenly.

But Jack said, "Frog, you're a genius . . ."

The frog grinned and went on. "Then there's an *s*, not a *j*, and that's two *o*'s after an *l*, not a *b* and an *o*."

Jill nodded wonderingly.

"Finally," said the frog, "that's not an *a*. It's a *u* and an *r*."

Jack and Jill studied the mirror.

Their eyes traveled down the silvered pane.

They stared at their reflections.

And Jack and Jill, staring into the Glass, suddenly realized what their quest had actually been for, and what they had really been seeking all this time. And at that very moment, they found it.

Wait!

What?

What just happened?

What had they been looking for? What did they find?

Is the mirror magic? What did it show them?

Look, kid. I'm just telling this story. I don't have all the answers. You gotta figure it out yourself.

"Um," said a voice. "Excuse me, but did that frog just talk?"

Jack and Jill and the frog all spun around. Elsie and her little sister stood at the edge of their clearing, staring at them.

"Oh, boy . . ." muttered the frog.

"Well . . ." said Jack, "yes."

"How?" said Elsie.

"Can I see?" asked her sister.

Jack looked at Jill. Jill looked at the frog. The frog shrugged.

"Come over here," Jill said. She patted a spot on the log beside her. "Meet our friend Frog. He can talk."

"Hello," said the frog.

"Hi," said both redheaded girls at once.

"You're amazing . . ." said Elsie's little sister.

The frog beamed.

"How do you talk?" Elsie asked.

"It's a long story," said the frog.

And both little girls, at the very same moment, said, "Okay."

The frog sighed.

The sun was setting, and the sky was red and yellow and pink and blue as the frog finished his story.

"That was wonderful . . ." Elsie said with a sigh.

"Can you tell it again?" asked Elsie's little sister.

Jack and Jill laughed.

"I mean, tomorrow," the little girl said. "I want to bring my friends."

The smiles slid off of Jack's and Jill's faces.

"Yeah," said Elsie. "All the kids will want to meet the frog now!"

"And hear the story!" her sister agreed.

Jack and Jill both looked at the frog. "What do you think?" said Jill.

The frog turned his head coyly to one side. "They'll *all* want to meet me?" he asked.

"Oh, yes!"

"A*nd* hear the story?"

"Definitely!"

ADAM GIDWITZ

"Well," the frog replied. "If you *insist*."

The next afternoon, all the children who had ever come to clearing to play with Jack and Jill were gathered before the hollow log. The frog sat between Jack and Jill. And once the children had gotten over their hysterical excitement about meeting a talking frog, he told them all his story.

He finished when the sky was dark, and the stars were twinkling overhead.

The children all instantly clamored for more: "What happened next? How did you meet Jack and Jill? Can we meet the salamanders?"

"No," the frog replied, "you can*not* meet the salamanders. And as for how I met Jack and Jill? That's another very long story."

And all the children, all at once, said, "Okay."

Jack and Jill laughed. And then Jill said, "Why don't we tell you tomorrow?"

The next day, an even larger group of children had assembled. Even some boys from Jack's village were there. Not Marie, of course. But some of the quieter ones.

Jill told them all about her mother and the silk merchant and the terrible royal procession.

The children adored it. They ate up every word. A little

boy in the back named Hans Christian laughed and gaped and clapped his hands straight the way through.

The day after, Jack told them about having to sell Milky and about the snake oil salesman. The boys from Jack's village laughed when Jack sang the Little Lamb song, and told the other children that it was all true—that there really was a rickety old cart, and Jack did trade his cow for a bean. And then Jack and Jill and the frog told them about the creepy old lady with the pale eyes and the beanstalk. The children were mesmerized. Especially a little boy sitting in the front named Joseph, but whom everyone called J.J.

After the story, as the stars were spinning in the dark sky, Elsie and her little sister pulled some of the boys from the village aside.

"Don't you think Jack's father misses him?" Elsie asked.

"He does," one of the boys replied. "He's in mourning."

"I bet Jill's mother misses her, too," said Elsie's little sister.

"Well," said Elsie, "why don't we find out?"

The next night, the group was enormous. Jack and Jill had planned to tell the giant story, and they had gathered enough sticks and branches to make a large fire. The children sat round the crackling flames as dusk settled in, and Jack and Jill and the frog prepared to tell them about their adventures in the sky.

But before they could begin, some dark figures approached

the back of the group. There were at least three of them, and they were pretty big for kids.

Elsie ran up to Jill and tugged on her arm. "Jill," she whispered. "Do you think you could tell us the story from the beginning again? Most of the kids here missed the frog's part." Jill shrugged and asked Jack. Jack shrugged and asked the frog. The frog shrugged and said, "They want to hear *my* story again? I don't know . . ."

He began his story again.

And off in the trees, a woman as tall as a statue and slender as a willow wand put her hand before her mouth and stared. Then she laughed. Then she grew serious. By the end of the story, she was wiping a tear from her eye.

The next evening, the crowd of children returned. And the next. And the next. And each evening, once the fire was raging and the children were comfortable, those three dark figures would come up behind the group and stand among the trees.

They heard about the silk merchant and the snake oil salesman and the old woman. They heard about the giants. They heard about Jack and Jill tumbling from the sky and falling down the hill.

A little girl sitting near the front, whose last name was Goose, laughed so hard at that part that Jack and Jill stopped telling the story and stared at her.

"I broke my head open," Jack reminded her.

"I know," said the little girl, wiping tears of mirth from her eyes. "I'm sorry."

They heard about the mermaid. They heard about the goblins. They heard about Eddie. Everyone loved Eddie. Finally, they heard about the terrible Others.

As Jack and Jill spoke, the fire illuminated their faces, igniting their features, flashing in their eyes. They spoke with such passion—and of such fearful and wondrous things. Their voices boomed and the children all sat back; their voices swooped down low and everyone leaned in. And Jack and Jill were fierce. And honest. And impressive. And beautiful. In the crackling light of the fire, out there in the pale green grove among the dark trees, everyone saw it. They were amazing, fierce, beautiful children.

And then they came to the final story. About returning home. They told it, and the tall figures in the back hugged their arms to their chests. They told about coming to live in these woods. And the friends they'd made.

And then they invited the frog to tell about the Seeing Glass—and his discovery. So he did.

He told them that what had seemed to say, "*Fo timb hat da jeek, bok no father,*" did not say that at all.

He told them that the *f* was actually a *t*.

308   ADAM GIDWITZ

He told them the *t* was an *f*.

He told them the *m* was a . . .

"Just tell us what it said!" someone cried.

"Oh!" said the frog. "Sure."

He cleared his throat.

"It said, 'To find what ye seek, look no further.'"

In the clearing, there was no sound but the crackling fire.

"What does that mean?" a child asked.

Jack smiled, and answered, "It means that it took a crazy quest, and almost dying lots of times, and more pain than anyone should ever have to go through—but we finally figured out what we'd been looking for all along."

"And," said Jill, "at that very moment, we found it."

"What *was* it?" a big boy shouted.

"It was right there in the Glass," Jill replied.

"What?" said Elsie. "What did you see?"

Jack smiled. "What do you think we saw? It's a mirror. We saw ourselves."

And then, suddenly, something burst inside of that tall, slender figure standing among the trees. She broke from the shadows and ran forward, over and through the seated children.

Jill stood up.

"Mom?" she said.

Her mother threw her arms around her. She whispered, "My beautiful, wise girl." Jack's father, and then the king, too, emerged from the trees, came up to the children, and embraced them.

Then the queen let go of Jill and turned to the frog—who was frozen, staring at her. And she said, "I owe you this," and she picked up the frog and kissed him. Right on the mouth. All the children broke out cheering. The frog, on the other hand, fainted.

The queen turned back to Jill, to embrace her again.

But Jill had turned away. She and Jack had put their arms around each other's shoulders, as best friends will do, and they were watching the black smoke from the bonfire rise into the sky. Overhead, the darkness was still littered with stars. But in the east, there were signs of dawn.

Wait, wait, go back.

Are you saying the Glass was just a mirror? It wasn't magic or anything?

No, I wouldn't say that. I'd say that all mirrors are magic, or can be.

They show you yourself, after all.

Really *seeing* yourself, though—that's the hard part.

———

Suddenly, a roar shook the forest. It was so loud that the leaves fell from branches, the earth shook, and an old tree fell over.

Everyone in the clearing doubled over and covered their ears. Their eyes were all panic. What was happening? Was the world coming to an end?

Jack and Jill were doubled over, too. But they were not panicked. They were laughing.

Once the roar had subsided, a giant head emerged from the darkness.

"Run!" someone screamed. "Run! It's a dragon!"

But it was not a dragon, of course. It was Eddie.

On top of Eddie's head sat the three ravens.

"Sorry to intrude," said the first raven.

"But this guy was lost," said the second.

Everyone around the bonfire stared at the talking birds, perched atop the head of the most enormous, foulest-smelling beast they could have ever imagined.

"He was looking for you," the third raven explained.

"Looking for us?" Jack asked.

"He's been looking for you for weeks now," the second raven said.

"Why?" demanded Jill. "Is everything all right?"

"Oh, I think so," said the first raven. "I think he just has some questions he'd like to ask you."

So everyone sat around the bonfire as the sun rose in the east, trying to define the word *in* for Eddie, and deciding who was smellier, Eddie or Fred. Not that they knew who Fred was. The queen put the frog on her knee. The boys from the village sat beside Elsie and her little sister. And Jack and Jill had their arms around each other's shoulders.

Perched far up above in a pine tree, the three ravens looked down upon the scene.

The third raven said, "Okay, I have a question. What happens next? To Jack and Jill?"

"Don't you know?" scoffed the second. "You see the future as well as we do."

"Yes," said the third. "But the future is very large, and it's hard to keep track of everything."

"When they grow up, they will share the throne of Märchen," said the second raven.

"But they'll marry other people," the first interjected.

"Right. And Eddie will lead their armies."

"Not that that they ever fight a war," said the first. "Who would want to fight Eddie?"

"True. And they will govern by the light of the Seeing Glass."

"Which just means," explained the first, "that they'll read the inscription from time to time, to remind themselves."

"Exactly. And they will be the greatest and wisest rulers in the history of the kingdom of Märchen."

"And," added the first raven, "they will live happily ever after."

The three ravens sat in silence for a while, watching Jack and Jill—who were stronger than giants, more beautiful than mermaids, cleverer than goblins, and fast-friends with a giant, fire-breathing salamander.

Finally, the third raven asked, "The end?"

And the second raven said, "The end."

And the first raven said, "The end."

And it is, indeed,

Where Do These Stories Come From?

Sometimes kids ask me where I get my ideas. My answer is always the same: I steal them. Every writer steals, and writers who work in folk traditions steal liberally. But we don't *just* steal.

For hundreds of generations, writers and storytellers have taken the threads of older tales and have rewoven them into new garments— new garments that reflect our hands and our visions, and that fit the children we know and care for. All writers do this, even today. We who write in folk traditions are just a little more transparent about it.

My first book, *A Tale Dark & Grimm*, took its inspiration from the tales of the Brothers Grimm, and I was, in that book, often quite faithful to those awesome (and bloody) stories—just as the Brothers Grimm were often (but not always) quite faithful in retelling the stories that they collected. I am far less faithful to my sources in *In a Glass Grimmly*. This is because many of these tales are *Kunstmärchen*, or "original" fairy tales—tales that were invented by a known author, like Hans Christian Andersen or Christina Rossetti. And what better way to be faithful to invented stories than inventing my own? So the plot, the themes, and the architecture of *In a Glass Grimmly* are wholly mine, as they were in *A Tale Dark & Grimm*. But this time, most of the chapters are wholly mine, too, with a wink and a nod here and there to those awesome story-weavers who came before me.

My chapter "The Wishing Well" is based on "The Frog King or Iron Heinrich," collected by the Brothers Grimm. It is the most faithful retelling in the book. The name of the kingdom, Märchen, is actually the German word for "fairy tales"—though "fairy tales" is a bad translation. Really it just means "stories you tell around your house if you want to scare the bejeezus out of everybody." The details about tears on water waking the stars, and the stars granting wishes, were also used in my first book, A Tale Dark & Grimm. Those details come from the Grimm tale "The Seven Ravens."

The chapter "The Wonderful Mother" is based, loosely, on Hans Christian Andersen's "The Emperor's New Clothes."

"Jack and Jill and the Beanstalk" is inspired by Joseph Jacobs's story "Jack and the Beanstalk," though I've changed just about everything in it. The chant "Marie had a little lamb" is a riff on the Mother Goose rhyme "Mary had a little lamb." (Sorry to belabor the obvious here.) Jack's rhyme about jumping over the candlestick is also from Mother Goose.

"The Giant Killer" is based, very loosely, on Joseph Jacobs's "Jack the Giant Killer." The setting and situations are quite different, but the tests, and Jill's ultimate solution, were suggested by Jacobs's text.

"Where You'll Never Cry No More" is inspired by Scottish and Irish legends of the water nixie, though no specific tales were drawn upon. Just my messed up imagination. The beginning of that chapter, when Jack and Jill fall from the sky and then down the hill, and Jack breaks his head open, is my homage to the Mother Goose rhyme "Jack and Jill."

"Goblin Market" is inspired by Christina Rossetti's brilliant poem of the same name, which I really wish I had written. The fruit sellers' chant is lifted directly from her poem.

"The Gray Valley" is original, though the three ravens, whom you might remember from A *Tale Dark & Grimm*, come from the Grimm tale "Faithful Johannes."

"Death or the Lady" is inspired by three sources. The first is Frank Stockton's original story, "The Lady or the Tiger," first published in 1882. It is unforgettable and highly recommended—but better for adults than kids. The second is the Jewish folk tale "The Grand Inquisitor," collected by Nina Jaffe and Steve Zeitlin in *While Standing on One Foot: Puzzle Stories and Wisdom Tales from the Jewish Tradition*; this story also appears in Nathan Ausubel's A *Treasury of Jewish Folklore*. The third source, where I first heard the riddle with the slips of paper and the casket, is a puzzler from the NPR show *Car Talk*—which was called "The Lady or the Tiger."

"The Descent" and "Eidechse von Feuer, der Menschenfleisch-fressende". are original. Jack's mumbling about all the king's horses and all the king's men is a reference to the Mother Goose rhyme "Humpty Dumpty." I must thank Chiara Frigeni for her help with my, shall we say, "creative" use of German in coming up with Eddie's full name.

The chapters "The Others" and "Face to Face" are also original. When Jack and Jill start into the kingdom of Märchen, I quote the Mother Goose verse, "Home again, home again, jiggedy jig." The rhyme "Mirror, mirror on the wall, who is the fairest of them all?" is from the Grimms' "Snow White." The rest of the mirror rhymes are invented. The Others' punishment, and the fact that they unwittingly choose it themselves, is drawn from the Grimm tale "The Three Woodsmen."

The book's inscription comes from the New Testament, 1 Corinthians 13:12: "We see now as in a glass, dimly, but then we shall see face to face." The book's title, and the title of the last chapter, and the whole structure of the book, reflect this verse.

Acknowledgments

First and foremost, I must acknowledge the immense importance of Julie Strauss-Gabel, the editor of *In a Glass Grimmly* and *A Tale Dark & Grimm*. Our process is this: I write a book that is meaningful to me, and then she tells me if anyone will have any idea what I'm talking about. She explains what works, what does not, and why. I rewrite. We repeat the process. Endlessly. Until the book I wanted to write has been revealed. She is throughout as generous to my vision as she is firm against my excesses. If my books convey any meaning to the reader at all, it is because of Julie.

I must also thank the wonderful people at Penguin. Scottie Bowditch in particular has guided my work from obscurity to recognition with the resolution and intuition of a brilliant sea captain. Liza Kaplan has taken care of all the behind scenes work. Bernadette Cruz and Marie Kent, together, have introduced me to half of the librarians and booksellers in the country—I can't wait to be introduced to the other half. The entire Penguin team does incredible work just to ensure that children get to read these stories; I am deeply grateful to them.

Sarah Burnes, my agent, guides my life as it relates to books as insightfully as Julie guides my writing. I would be utterly and totally lost without her. And without Logan Garrison, too. Rebecca Gardner and Will Roberts at The Gernert Company have gotten *A Tale Dark & Grimm* into more languages and countries than I can keep track of; they are masters.

Hugh D'Andrade's incredible covers and interior art deserve their own gallery show. Perhaps we'll arrange that one day. For now, the fantastic work of the Penguin Young Readers Group design team will do nicely.

Laura Amy Schlitz was my elementary school librarian, and it may be that I learned the art of storytelling by watching her masterful, weekly performances. More recently, she has taken me under her wing, offering endless advice, comfort, and care through the process of becoming, and being, a writer. I do not deserve her.

I feel deep gratitude toward Sal Vascellero of the Bank Street College of Education, as well as toward Amy Hest. Both Sal and Amy guided me through my very first attempts at writing, and were endlessly encouraging when I needed encouragement most.

Zachary Gidwitz and Lauren Mancia both read drafts of this book and improved it immensely with their honesty.

My family and my close friends are more important to me than anything else in the world. I know that you guys know that, but I just wanted to tell you again.

Finally, I've got to say thank you to the kids. You know who you are. All the kids to whom I've told stories, at every school and library and bookstore I've visited—and, of course, at Saint Ann's. Your laughter, your shrieks of horror, and your enduring passion for stories are . . . well . . . awesome.

Turn the page for a teaser
of the companion to
In a Glass Grimmly—

A *Tale Dark & Grimm*

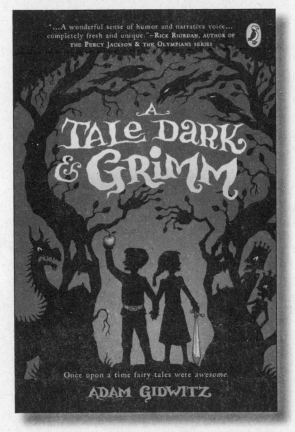

. . . if you dare.

*O*nce upon a time, in a kingdom called Grimm, an old king lay on his deathbed. He was Hansel and Gretel's grandfather—but he didn't know that, for neither Hansel nor Gretel had been born yet.

Now hold on a minute.

I know what you're thinking.

I am well aware that nobody wants to hear a story that happens *before* the main characters show up. Stories like that are boring, because they all end exactly the same way. With the main characters showing up.

But don't worry. This story is like no story you've ever heard.

You see, Hansel and Gretel don't just *show up* at the end of this story.

They show up.

And then they get their heads cut off.

Just thought you'd like to know.

The old king knew he was soon to pass from this world, and so he called for his oldest and most faithful servant. The servant's name was Johannes; but he had served the king's father, and his father's father, and his father's father's father so loyally that all called him Faithful Johannes.

Johannes tottered in on bowed legs, heaving his crooked back step by step and leering with his one good eye. His long nose sniffed at the air. His mouth puckered around two rotten teeth. But, despite his grotesque appearance, when he came within view, the old king smiled and said, "Ah, Johannes!" and drew him near.

The king's voice was weak as he said, "I am soon to die. But before I go, you must promise me two things. First, promise that you will be as faithful to my young son as you have been to me."

Without hesitation, Johannes promised.

The old king went on. "Second, promise that you will show him his entire inheritance—the castle, the treasures, all this fine land—*except* for one room. Do not show him the room with the portrait of the golden princess. For if he sees the portrait he will fall madly in love with her. And I fear it will cost him his life."

The king gripped Johannes's hand. "Promise me."

Again Johannes promised. Then the wrinkles of worry left the king's brow, and he closed his eyes and breathed his last.

Soon the prince was crowned as the new king. He was celebrated with parades and toasts and feasts all throughout the kingdom. But, when the revelry finally abated, Johannes sat him down for a talk.

First, Johannes described to him all of the responsibilities of the throne. The young king tried not to fall asleep.

Then he explained that the old king had asked him to show the young king his entire inheritance—the castle, the treasures, all this fine land. At the word *treasures* the young king's face lit up. Not that he was greedy. It was just that he found the idea of treasures exciting.

Finally, Johannes tried to explain his own role to the young king. "I have served your father, and your father's father, and your father's father's father before that," Johannes said. The young king started calculating on his fingers how that was even possible, but before he could get very far, Johannes had moved on. "They call me Faithful Johannes because I have devoted my life to the Kings of Grimm. To helping them. To advising them. To under-standing them."

"Understanding them?" the young king asked.

"No. Under-standing them. In the ancient sense of the word. Standing beneath them. Supporting them. Bearing their troubles and their pains on my shoulders."

The young king thought about this. "So you will under-stand me, too?" he asked.

"I will."

"No matter what?"

"Under any circumstances. That is what being faithful means."

"Well, under-stand that I am tired of this, and would like to see the treasures now." And the young king stood up.

Faithful Johannes shook his head and sighed.

They began by exploring every inch of the castle—the treasure crypts, the towers, and every single room. Every single room, that is, save one. One room remained locked, no matter how many times they passed it.

Well, the young king was no fool. He noticed this. And so he asked, "Why is it, Johannes, that you show me every room in the palace, but never *this* room?"

Johannes squinted his one good eye and curled up his puckered, two-toothed mouth. Then he said, "Your father asked me not to show you that room, Your Highness. He feared it might cost you your life."

I'm sorry, I need to stop for a moment. I don't know what you're thinking right now, but when I first heard this part of the story, I thought, "What, is he crazy?"

Maybe you know something about young people, and maybe you don't. I, having been one myself once upon a time, know a few things about them. One thing I know is that if you don't want one to do something—for example, go into a room where there's a portrait of an unbearably beautiful princess—saying "It might cost you your life" is about the *worst* thing you could possibly say. Because then that's *all* that young person will want to do.

I mean, why didn't Johannes say something else? Like, "It's a broom closet. Why? You want to see a broom closet?" Or, "It's a fake door, silly. For decoration." Or even, "It's the ladies' bathroom, Your Majesty. Best not go poking your head in there."

Any of those would have been perfectly sufficient, as far as I can tell.

But he didn't say any of those things. If he had, none of the horrible, bloody events to follow would ever have happened.

(Well, in that case, I guess I'm glad he told the truth.)

"Cost me my life?!" the young king proclaimed with a toss of his head. "Nonsense!" He insisted he be let into the room. First he demanded. But Johannes refused. Then he commanded. Still Johannes refused. Then he threw himself on the floor and had a fit, which was very unbecoming for a young man the king's age. Finally, Faithful Johannes realized there was little he could do. So, wrinkling his old, malformed face into a wince, he unlocked and opened the door.

The king burst into the room. He found himself staring, face-to-face with the most beautiful portrait of the most beautiful woman he had ever seen in his life. Her hair looked like it was spun from pure gold thread. Her eyes flashed like the ocean on a sunny day. And yet, around her lips, there was a hint of sadness, of loneliness.

The young king took one look at her and fainted dead away.

———

ADAM GIDWITZ

Later, in his room, he came to. Johannes hovered over his bed. "Who was that radiant creature?" the king asked.

"That, Your Majesty, is the golden princess," Johannes answered.

"She's the most beautiful woman in the world," the young king said.

And Johannes answered, "Yes, she is."

"And yet she looked almost sad. Why is that?"

Johannes took a deep breath, and replied, "Because, young king, she is cursed. Every time she has tried to marry, her husband has died; and it is said that a fate worse than death is destined for her children, if ever she should have any. She lives in a black marble palace, topped with a golden roof, all by herself. And, as you can imagine, she is terribly lonely and terribly sad."

The king sat straight up in his bed and grabbed the front of Faithful Johannes's tunic. And though he stared into the old man's face, he saw only the princess's ocean-bright eyes and her lips ringed with sadness. "I must have her," he said. "I will marry her. I will save her."

"You may not survive," Johannes said.

"I will survive, if you help me. If you are faithful to me, if you under-stand me, you'll do it."

Johannes feared for the young king's life. But he had understood the young king's father, and his father's father, and his father's father's father before that. What could he say?

Johannes sighed. "I'll do it."

It was widely known that in all the golden princess's days of loneliness, the only thing that gave her any modicum of happiness was gold. So Johannes told the king to gather all of the gold in the kingdom and to command his goldsmiths to craft the most exquisite golden objects that the world had ever seen. Which soon was done.

Then Johannes disguised himself and the king as merchants and loaded a ship with the golden goods. And they set off for the land of the golden princess.

As their ship's prow split the sea, Johannes tutored the king in his part: "You're a gold merchant, Your Majesty. The princess has always loved gold, but these days, it is the only thing that gives her any joy. So when I bring her to the ship, charm her not only with your gentle manners and fine looks, but also with the gold. Then, perhaps, she will be yours."

When they landed, the king readied the ship and tended to his merchant costume, while Johannes, carrying a few golden objects in his bag, made his way to the towering ramparts of black marble where the golden princess lived. He entered the courtyard, and there discovered a serving girl retrieving water from a well with a golden bucket.

"Pretty maid," he said, smiling his kind but unhandsome smile, "do you think your lady might be interested in such trifling works of gold as these?" And he produced two of the finest, most exquisite golden statuettes that man's hand has ever made.

The girl was stunned by their beauty. She took them from Johannes and hurried within. Not ten minutes had elapsed before the golden princess herself emerged from the castle, holding the statuettes in her hands. She was as gorgeous as her portrait—more so in fact—and as she greeted Johannes, her golden hair flashed in the light and her ocean-blue eyes danced with pleasure. Still, around her lips there was sadness.

"Tell me, old man," she said, "are these really for sale? I've never seen anything so beautiful, so fine."

Faithful Johannes bowed. "But there is more, fair princess, much more. My master's ship is full of such wonders. And they can be yours, if you will just accompany me down to the harbor."

The princess hesitated for a moment—since her last husband-to-be had died, she had not set foot outside the palace. But the allure of the gold was too strong. She threw a shining traveling cloak over her shoulders and followed Johannes to the boat.

The young king, in his disguise as a merchant, greeted her.

Her beauty was so stunning, her sadness so apparent and so tender, that he nearly fainted again. But somehow he did not, and she smiled at him and invited him to show her all the treasures he had brought to her fair land.

As soon as they had descended below the deck, Johannes hurried to the captain of the ship, and, in whispered tones, instructed him to cast off from shore and set sail for home immediately.

Now, my young readers, I know just what you're thinking. You're thinking, *Hmmm. Stealing a girl. That's an* interesting *way of winning her heart.* Allow me to warn you now that, under any other circumstances, stealing a girl is about the worst way of winning her heart you could possibly cook up.

But, because this happened long ago, in a faraway land, it seems to have worked.

For the golden princess came back up to the deck and saw that her land was far away from her. At first she did indeed protest, and fiercely, too, that she'd been carried away by lowborn merchants. But when one of the "merchants" revealed himself to be a king, and revealed that, in addition, he was madly in love with her, and when, besides, Johannes assured her that, if she *really* wanted to, she could go home, but she couldn't take the gold if she did, the princess realized that in fact the young king was just the kind of man she would like to marry after all, and decided that she'd give the whole matrimony thing one last shot.

And they all lived happily ever after.

The End

And don't miss
the thrilling,
chilling finale . . .

The Grimm Conclusion

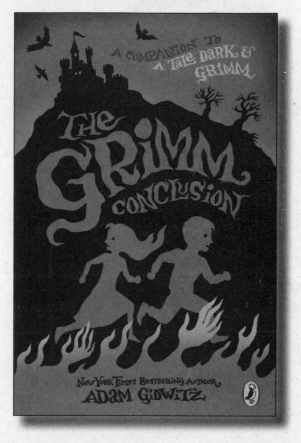